EL TIGRE AZUL:

# Three Witches
*Expanded Edition*

Duane Spurlock

INTERROBANG TALES / LOUISVILLE, KENTUCKY

**InterroBang Tales**
**Louisville, Kentucky**
**www.duanespurlock.com**

Publisher's Note: This is a work of fiction. Names, characters, places, and incidents are a product of the author's imagination. Locales and public names are sometimes used for atmospheric purposes. Any resemblance to actual people, living or dead, or to businesses, companies, events, institutions, or locales is completely coincidental.

Cover art by Jeffrey Ray Hayes
InterroBang Tales colophon by J.T. Lindroos
Book Layout © 2017 BookDesignTemplates.com

**El Tigre Azul: Three Witches – Expanded Edition / Duane Spurlock**. -- 1st ed.
Print edition
ISBN 979-8-9877970-0-6

*Dedication to Jim Beard:*
*Persistence and Perseverance*


*The battleline between good and evil runs through the heart of*
*every man.*

— ALEKSANDR SOLZHENITSYN, *THE GULAG ARCHIPELAGO*

# CONTENTS

# { 1 }

# Three Witches

*Tres Brujas*

CHAPTER ONE

El Tigre Azul had his hands full.

He grabbed The Pinky and wrenched to the left, then the right.

He stomped The Ring with a boot heel.

The Middle was jammed between a door frame and its slammed door: solid wood, encased in steel.

He whacked The Pointer with a pool cue—left, right, left, until the stick broke.

That left The Thumb.

Came a shout from the adjoining room: "The Fingers are nothing without The Thumb!"

El Pulgar leaped into the pool room through the back doorway. He was accompanied by the staccato-strobe of powder flash from the Thompson submachine gun tucked into the crook of his arm. The Thumb advanced into the room as .45 slugs gouged holes in the plaster walls, smashed splinters from the intricately carved wooden tables, chewed the felt and cracked the slate beds. Balls were blown to powder, bottles of beer and liquor on and behind the bar shattered and fell to the floor in a torrent loud as Niagra Falls. Clouds of dust—from exploding plaster, felt, and chalk—billowed and dropped visibility in the room to near nil, worsened by the light dancing from the chain-hung fixtures swinging this way and that as it was knocked by ricocheting bullets.

The machine gun's chattering racket ceased only for seconds as El Pulgar replaced the empty clip with a fresh stack of live loads. He swung the weapon's line of fire to the left, where he had heard a skittering during the momentary silence—the sound of El Tigre Azul moving to fresh cover from the storm of lead.

The Thumb let up on the Tommy gun's trigger. He listened in the sudden hush.

Where had The Blue Tiger gone?

El Pulgar was nearly five feet tall only because he wore boots with tall heels. Black hair curled on the backs of his hands, his eyebrows were thick, and his pomaded hair atop his head was spiked in different directions like the tail of a riled rooster. He wore a tweed vest open over a white shirt whose starched front was marred with grimy spots. His trousers matched his vest.

His black eyes turned. As the gunsmoke thinned and the dust settled, he scanned the room for likely hiding places. A flame danced on one of the tables—the green baize ignited by the machine gun's powder flash—and threw frets of light across El Pulgar's twisted features. He climbed on a chair and looked behind the bar. He climbed up on the bartop. An overturned table at the far end of the room was a possibility. El Pulgar made a slow turn. A typewriter sitting on the bar—at its far end—caught his eye for a moment. It was an object that seemed completely out of place here. Somehow, amazingly, it had escaped the torrent of gunfire entirely unscathed. The Thumb continued surveying the bar for The Blue Tiger.

This typewriter is worth a few words. It was a Royal Model KMM, manufactured in 1939. It stood in a position almost of reverence at the center of a philosophical movement.

The movement was small, embracing fewer than one hundred people. But they were devoted. For fifty years, Hector Ruiz Costas Velez— owner of the billiard parlor that now appeared a shambles—had dedicated hours of each day to promoting the play of billiards as the key to inner peace and outward calm. On this very Royal typewriter he had hammered out on untold reams of paper rolled by its platen thousands and hundreds of thousands of words about the crisp rolling of tapped spheres across smooth expanses of green felt paradise. These words then were retyped on stencils and run through a hand-cranked mimeograph machine, and the reproductions mailed to fervent readers in three countries.

Before Hector began to type, he would caress the sides of the Royal, close his eyes and picture in his mind an endless stretch of perfect green felt. He understood the grace within the Royal, how it represented the ingenuity of men who could bring to realization the notion of moving words effortlessly from the mind to the virgin white of a sheet of paper—how cold metal could dance at the whim of a man's fingers to create wonder from a strip of ink-impregnated fabric. He would lightly touch the space bar with his fingertips before addressing the home keys. The Royal, Hector knew, was simpatico with his vision of a world at peace with spheres upon the flawless green.

El Pulgar knew nothing of Hector and his love for his inanimate machine of ingenious design. He craned his neck, looking for The Blue Tiger. Spotted the Fingers where they lay unconscious after having been thrashed by El Tigre Azul. The Pinky, The Ring, The Middle, The

Pointer—all had failed him and his plans. The Thumb snarled and pulled the trigger.

Blood and fabric erupted from their torsos. Their bodies danced a gavotte of death to the Tommy gun's heartless rhythm.

El Tigre Azul popped up from the corner of the bar where he had been hidden. His left hand whipped out, snagged the Royal Model KMM, and hurled all sixteen pounds of it.

The typewriter smashed into the chest of The Thumb. As he tumbled off the bar, the Thompson machine gun spewed an arc of fire. Bullets flew through the body of the typewriter. El Pulgar slammed to the floor, unconscious. The Royal crashed to pieces beside him.

In the sudden silence, El Tigre looked at the mess surrounding him. One last, unbroken beer mug teetered and fell from a shelf and broke on the pile of rubble below.

The wrestler advanced to the still bodies of The Fingers. He checked each. All were dead. He flipped over The Ring, pulled a Colt .45 automatic from the bloody thug's shoulder holster.

El Tigre Azul's right hand and right ankle were shackled together with a two-foot chain. He shot through the links with the pistol.

He stretched his back, then pulled belts from two of the dead men. He used these to bind The Thumb to a pool table's ornately carved leg. Then he opened the front door. Three men rushed out of the daylight glare into the smoke-filled wreck.

The first man in was Hector Ruiz Costas Velez. He gazed, shocked, at the ruin he saw. Only an hour ago he had walked out of his billiard parlor. It had looked nothing like this. He had hunkered behind a battered Ford parked on the street when he heard the sounds of gunpowder-fueled bedlam erupting from his place of business.

Then Hector saw the spot on the bar reserved for his favored Royal. The site, now bare.

He looked here, there. Then he saw it. His beloved machine of engineered grace.[1] Destroyed, beside the belt-trussed El Pulgar.

Hector's features, usually placid with an inner delight, scowled. Blood suffused his face. His teeth showed in a grimace. While El Tigre Azul used the telephone in the back room to call the police, Hector picked up the Thompson machine gun from the floor, pointed it at The Thumb, and pulled the trigger. He fired all fourteen of the loads that remained in the magazine.

The Blue Tiger rushed in, snatched the empty gun from Hector's twitching hands. He looked at El Pulgar and shook his head. "That's not good."


CHAPTER TWO

El Tigre Azul didn't arrive home until after midnight. The clock on the stove read two o'clock.

It wasn't even his home. He was house-sitting for his eighty-year-old aunt, who was snorkeling off the coast of Cozumel, jumping into the water from a sail boat each day. He still wore the remnants of the clothes in which he had started the previous morning: suit pants, a starched blue shirt, a solid ruby-red silk tie. The suit coat had been shredded during the course of his adventures against the members of The Hand. The shirt was stained and ripped. Half the necktie was missing. The trousers were missing the knees from each leg.

The Thumb was taken to the hospital in an ambulance under police guard. Hector's shots hadn't killed the evil little man, but he was grievously wounded.

Hector was escorted to jail in a police cruiser. The billiard saloon owner who had calmly recommended a quest for inner peace by contemplating the quiet geometries of small balls rolling smoothly across felt-dressed slate now snarled and snapped like a savage animal trapped in the wild. The police restrained Hector with shackles and locked him to D-rings bolted to the floor of the car.

The Blue Tiger had spent the rest of the day and much of the night responding to questions from investigators. He had driven to his aunt's house along streets that were deserted but for a few cats.

El Tigre didn't even turn on the lights. He pulled off his wingtip shoes in the kitchen, walked into the living room, switched on the television, and sat in the recliner. He pulled the chair's lever and lay back.

The TV set was fitted with rabbit ears, and the only thing it brought in at this time of night—more correctly, morning—was electrified snow. The volume was turned low, so the room was filled with a suffused hiss like sleet blown against a window.

El Tigre Azul was tired. Had he been less tired, he may have thought about the telephone that resided on a lamp table beside the recliner and taken it off the hook. But he just closed his eyes, so that his blue-and-black striped mask appeared sightless, and began to snore.

A gap between the closed blinds and the window sill allowed a bit of space for a pair of eyes to peer into the room at the sleeping wrestler from outside the house. In the television glow, El Tigre Azul's mask seemed to glow with phosphorescence in the dark.

Thirty minutes later, the telephone jangled. El Tigre Azul jerked awake, snatched up the receiver. "Who is it?"

"Good morning, Nephew."

"Auntie!" The wrestler rubbed his eyes. "Why are you calling at this time of night?"

"It's morning, Nephew."

"Why are you calling? What's wrong? Are you hurt?"

"Nothing is wrong. I call during the day, no one ever answers. So I call at night, when I suppose you've had enough time to settle down from all that wrestling and sweating you do during the day and evening."

"Okay, all right," he said. "Do you need something?"

"No. Is everything okay at the house?"

"Everything is fine."

"Wonderful. I'm calling to remind you to take out the garbage on Thursday. Thursday morning. Or Wednesday night."

"Auntie, it's Sunday night."

"Monday morning."

"Right, Monday morning. There is plenty of time to take out the garbage."

"I just thought about it and know how you don't plan ahead very well. I'm helping you to plan ahead."

"All right, thank you, Auntie. I'll take out the garbage."

"Very good."

"Can I go to sleep now?"

"Why are you up at this hour, anyway? You need your rest."

"Yes, yes, you're right, Auntie."

"Of course I am."

"Are you enjoying your snorkeling?"

"Absolutely. Now stop trying to distract me from scolding you. It's past your bedtime, young man."

"Yes, ma'am. Good night."

"Good morning, you mean." *Click!*

"Good morning," he said to the humming in his ear, and he replaced the receiver on its cradle. Two minutes later, El Tigre Azul was asleep again.

Forty minutes later, the telephone rang again.

The wrestler awoke and snatched up the receiver. "Auntie?"

"No, you dope, it's Ramon." Ramon arranged wrestling matches. "What are you doing up this time of night?"

"It's morning."

"So it is? It's still no time for you to be up and around."

"So why are you calling me?"

"In case you were awake. And you are, so stop arguing and listen. I have a match for you."

"Great. I'll be there."

"Wonderful. Are you still living with your Aunt?"

"I'm not living with my Aunt. I'm staying at her house while she is on a trip."

"Fine. So, you're at the aunt's house. You better leave soon."

"Why?"

"The match starts at ten in the morning."

"What?"

"Actually, ten this morning."

"Are you loco? Am I dreaming?"

"It'll take you about three hours to drive here."

"No, I'm not crazy. You are. I'm not doing it."

"It's a special match, for charity, for kids in the orphan home. Thirty minutes in the ring, you're done, and the kids have earned a bunch of money from selling tickets."

"Ugh, all right. But why not move the match to the evening? Or the next day?"

"The kids have already sold the tickets. Been selling them two days. Everybody is excited. 'El Tigre Azul!' Everyone in town is shouting your name."

"So? What about the evening? A few hours later, it's the same day, and I get a little more sleep."

"I've already booked you for the evening."

"The same day? Two matches the same day?"

"Sure."

"More charity?"

"Absolutely."

"'Absolutely.'" El Tigre sighed. "All the tickets already sold?"

"Absolutely."

"Hmmph. Can't all the evening ticket holders come to the morning match?"

"Different charity. School for disabled and very, very, very sick children. They have a kind of rivalry with the orphans. There might be a riot with the backers for the hospital school and the backers for the orphans if you showed up for only one event."

"Ramon, you're making me very tired."

"Hey, it's not me. You should be in bed by now."

El Tigre growled.

"But you better skip bed and start packing. You've got a three-hour drive ahead of you and a couple of wrestling matches."

The wrestler growled again.

"But tell you what, I'll treat you to a great meal and a wonderful massage and a nap between the two matches, how's that?" He rattled off the address for the morning event, then hung up without saying goodbye.

The Blue Tiger growled once more at the receiver, then hung it up. He shook his head and closed his eyes. Four minutes and twenty-three seconds later, his snoring covered the hissing from the TV. His mask glowed in the dark until a sliver of the dawn's light sliced into the room through the gap under the window blinds.

CHAPTER THREE

A children's show about puppets was playing on the television when El Tigre Azul awoke. He didn't mind puppets. But his night's lack of sleep made it difficult for him to find any appreciation for the puppets' antics.

His aunt's next-door neighbor was a man named Otis from the town of Orient in the state of Ohio. The wrestler knocked on Otis' door. While he waited, he looked down at his feet. A dead mouse was curled there, left by Otis's cat. El Tigre stepped aside.

The neighbor answered wearing flannel pajamas. "*Hola*, El Tigre." Otis had thick black hair and his face had not yet been shaved for the day. The bristles on his face and chin didn't help his looks. The neighborhood already gossiped about him because of his features: his cheek bones and chin were knobby protuberances, and his eyes bugged out. Otis tended toward gauntness, and his knobby-and-buggy face had frightened one small child who lived on the next street. One of the old widows who lived nearby told the grocer, "He looks like death warmed over." The gossips said there were stores in the state of Ohio the size of football stadiums, and the parking lots were big as towns. Someone suggested Otis had picked up his starved, scary looks while wandering lost among the blazing chrome of parked cars that surrounded the giant stores of Ohio.[2]

Otis had helped El Tigre Azul make repairs on his aunt's house, and he didn't think Otis was so weird. In turn, he had helped Otis find his lost cat, and the next day the wrestler had stepped out of the house to see Otis washing and waxing his Thunderbird.

This morning, El Tigre needed Otis' help.

"Good morning. I'm sorry to wake you, but I need to ask a favor."

"Sure."

"Can you drive me to a wrestling match? It's three hours away, and I need to sleep on the way."

"I don't know, Tiger."

"You can drive my Thunderbird."

"Okay, give me ten minutes."

Twelve minutes later, Otis was driving El Tigre Azul's powder-blue Thunderbird down the highway from town. The car's owner had a pillow tucked between his head and shoulder and was snoring.

Otis smiled all the while he drove. Handling the Thunderbird was like driving a rocket ship on the highway. The radio was off, but he nodded his head to some sort of space music he heard in his mind.

An hour away from their destination, El Tigre woke up and directed Otis to turn off the road to a small eatery. As the two men approached the door, a family with six shouting children came out. The last one out, the father, was turning to lock the door when the wrestler interrupted: "Can we get something to eat?"

The father nearly jumped in surprise when he saw who was addressing him. "El Tigre Azul! We are just leaving to see you fight!"

The wrestler laughed. "I'll need some food and coffee if I must stay on my feet during the match."

The father rubbed his chin. "We don't want to be late for the fight."

"They can't have a fight without me."

"You're right! Come in, come in, we'll fix you right up." The six shouting children rushed back into the building and surrounded the wrestler. He wrote his autograph on napkins and comic books for the kids. After he and Otis ate, the father filled up a Thermos of coffee for The Blue Tiger. On a short-order ticket, the wrestler wrote a note:

Front row seats for my friends.

He signed it and thanked the family for their hospitality and fine food.

Back in the car and full of nourishment, Otis hit the gas pedal and roared down the road. He began to hum. El Tigre recognized the tune as one sung by Bobby Darin. He started to sing. Otis joined in. An old man stood beside the road and pulled at his whiskers when he heard two voices singing "Beyond the Sea" over the roaring of the Thunderbird's engine as it blew past.

El Tigre directed Otis with the information he'd received over the phone from Ramon. They parked behind a school gymnasium, and the wrestler walked around to the front doors, where a line of ticket holders stretched past the corner. One youngster grabbed his hand and yelled, "Look, look, El Tigre Azul! I won the contest! I drew the poster for your match!"

The poster was taped to the wall beside the doors and featured a crude but brightly colored painting of The Blue Tiger fighting an octopus.

The boy said, "It's not as good as your usual posters, but I did it myself."

"It's a fine picture," the wrestler said. "It's full of raw energy and excitement! You did a wonderful job. But I didn't know I was fighting an octopus."

"Oh no," the boy said, "that is just a picture. I thought it was very exciting."

"And so it is."

El Tigre Azul changed in the locker room and went out to the floor of the gym where a ring had been erected. Nearly five hundred people sat on bleachers and folding chairs arranged on the floor.

A roar filled the gymnasium when the crowd caught sight of the fighter—a roar from five hundred human throats. The Blue Tiger's opponent—a wrestler who didn't wear a mask—already was hopping and warming up in the ring.

The two men met in the center of the ring and shook hands.

"I'm El Tigre Azul."

"I know who you are," his opponent said as they shook. He was a young man with broad shoulders. He had curly black hair and startling eyes the color of transparent Caribbean waters. He was a handsome fellow with a strong jaw, but his looks were marred by his sullen expression. El Tigre could hear the voices of many young girls calling out his opponent's name. "I am Reynaldo Rey. I fight you for the honor of the orphanage."

"It is a pleasure to meet you."

"It will be a pleasure to defeat you!" Rey did not smile. He stalked off to his corner. He waved to the crowd, and the audience—primarily its female members—cheered their local hero.

The match soon commenced. The two men circled, each keeping wary eyes on the other. Then, with a sudden lunge, the wrestlers grappled. Cheers and whistles and shrieks from the audience banged around the building's rafters and back to the ring where the fighters sweated and grunted.

Each time El Tigre managed to grip Rey, his opponent slipped from his grasp and grabbed him in retaliation with a remarkably vicious hold.

The Blue Tiger rolled and flung Rey from him. He turned and grabbed Rey, who flipped and whipped back to his feet, dislodging his opponent. As the men focused on their battle, the sounds of the crowd disappeared from their conscious minds, replaced only with the thumps and shudders vibrating the fighting ring floor and ropes.

The image flashed into El Tigre's mind of the child's poster he'd seen before entering the building. He thought Rey's ability to escape holds and latch onto his opponent might rightly allow him to be named The Octopus.

Rey snarled and slammed into El Tigre, who tumbled to the mat. Rey leaped atop his opponent, smacked the masked head against the floor, and pinned his shoulders. All the while he growled imprecations against El Tigre Azul.

Crime fighting El Pulgar and the Fingers the previous day had winded El Tigre Azul. He had intended to allow the local fighter a good showing before the charity crowd, but the man's ill nature and bad manners were as irritating as beach sand in one's pajamas.

El Tigre Azul had had enough.

His body surged like a wave beneath Rey, throwing off the young fighter. The masked man was on his feet in a second, and anyone in the audience would have said he appeared to fly. He snagged the stumbling Rey by the neck and waist and flung the arrogant fellow against the ropes.

Rey bounded back to the ring's center, where El Tigre snatched him in mid-stagger, twirled him around in a graceful move that would have raised the envy of competitive ice skaters. He pitched the youth against the ropes again. As Rey ricocheted back to his opponent, The Blue Tiger bent, caught Rey on his shoulder, then lifted and tossed the young man head over heels.

El Tigre pinned Rey's shoulders. He was counted out, the match ended, and the crowd screamed its delight at the match's dramatic finish.

Rey lay on the mat and snarled like an angry dog, ignored by the mob shouting the victor's name. He kicked his heels against the mat. No one gave him their attention. El Tigre left his opponent behind, stepped down from the ring. He signed a few autographs, then was escorted by a local cop to the locker room.

When he emerged, he no longer wore his dazzling leggings and boots, although his mask was still in place. He had put on a white guayabera over chinos. The gym was empty. Even Rey was gone. He walked out the front door, where a small mob surrounded a table. Sitting there was Ramon, selling glossy photos of El Tigre Azul. An autograph was scrawled across the bottom of each photo. The wrestler shook his head. The signature looked nothing like his own.

He waited. The small crowd was stymied in its efforts to acquire glossies while Ramon chatted with a delicately curved young woman. She smiled coyly and batted her lashes when Ramon made a joke. Finally the girl trotted away. When Ramon ran out of glossies, he shooed away the remaining fans, then stood and shook his client's hand. "Great! Great! That Reynaldo is a nasty fellow. The girls say he is handsome, but even his fans don't like him. You were too easy on him."

El Tigre shrugged. "I'm hungry. You promised me a meal and a massage."

"Sure, sure, come along. There's a new place to eat down the street. We can walk. Great food." He slapped the wrestler on the back. "Great fight! Great fight!"

"Hey, wait a minute." El Tigre walked around to the back of the gym. Otis was sitting on the ground, his back leaned against the driver's side front hub cap on the Thunderbird. He was smoking a cigarette and reading a comic book: *El Hombre Enmascarado*. The cover depicted in garish colors a muscular man dressed in purple and wearing a mask. He was wrestling a gorilla.

"Hey, Otis, Ramon's going to treat us to some food."

Otis hopped up, dropped the book onto the car seat, and joined his neighbor and Ramon on their walk to the restaurant.

Otis said, "Don't you think The Phantom gets hot and sweaty running around the jungle in his long johns?"

Neither of his companions responded.

Ramon eyed Otis. Ramon had wavy pomaded hair combed back from his face and a crisply trimmed mustache. He was dressed in an immaculately tailored blue suit and a silk tie. He stood five-two and wore shoe inserts to make him taller. He never left his home until he was suitably dapper.

By comparison, Otis was tall, lanky, disheveled. The knobby features of his face made him look untrustworthy, a characteristic enhanced by the unshaven bristles scattered like iron filings across his chin and jaws. His shirt was wrinkled and open at the collar, and the tail was half out of the waistband of his pants, which carried no crease—or any crease was outnumbered by wrinkles. He wore sneakers, like a youth would, but Otis clearly was in his thirties.

Otis didn't smell, but only Ramon's veneer of courtesy kept him from pinching his nose while looking at Otis.

He admitted, however, that Otis would offer no competition for the attentions of attractive *chicas*.

Ramon led the way to a storefront and entered. The sign above the door read *TEXAS PANCAKE HOUSE.*

The three sat at a table. There were no other customers. El Tigre turned his head this way and that. "What is this place?"

Ramon smiled. "The Texas Pancake House. Very good."

A woman wearing an apron came through a door in the back. She placed four plates on the table, one in front of each man, and one in the middle of the table. Piled on the middle plate were half-a-dozen slices of ham. The plates before the men each held a stack of pancakes and a slathering of butter spilling from the top cake.

"What is this, Ramon?" El Tigre Azul glared across the table.

Otis picked up a knife and fork and tucked in.

Ramon smiled. "Eat up, all you can eat. I said I would feed you, right?"

"Ramon, I've been up most the night and I've fought a mean little El Pulpo and I've got another fight tonight and I'm ready for a steak!"

Ramon kept smiling. Even as he began to stuff pancake pieces into his mouth. "Eat all the ham you want. Good as steak."

Otis nodded. "It's good."

The Blue Tiger held his glare for thirty more seconds. Ramon and Otis continued to eat, undisturbed by the wrestler's disgust. Finally, the masked man growled and began to eat.

CHAPTER FOUR

An hour later, the trio stood outside the Texas Pancake House.

"You owe me a massage," El Tigre Azul said. The tone of his voice lacked a timbre of sated happiness.

"And you'll get one," Ramon said. His hands made gestures meant to placate the wrestler. "But it's a bad idea to get a massage on a full belly. You want a nap, right? Rest up for the evening's bout?"

El Tigre grunted a noise that could have been interpreted as an affirmative response.

They walked some more. Ramon led them to a residential street. The character of the houses steadily declined in respectability as they continued. Finally Ramon approached a structure that could only be called a shack. He knocked on the door.

El Tigre Azul looked at Otis. Otis was focused on lighting a cigarette.

A woman answered the door. The top of her head didn't even reach Ramon's shoulder. The skin of her face was flaccid like that of an old balloon that had lost its air. Wrinkles upon wrinkles surrounded her eyes, but those eyes were black like polished marbles and displayed a sharp intelligence.

The old woman seemed to know Ramon, and soon as she lay eyes on him invited the three into her home. Despite the external signs of disrepair, the interior was tidy and clean.

The woman kept up her silence. She left the room.

Ramon spread his hands. "You can nap here."

After a few moments, Otis raised his eyebrows and looked at the wrestler. Even he noted the pregnant pause before El Tigre responded: "Is there a bed?"

Ramon smiled. "Yes, but oh, you can't sleep there. No man has slept there since she gave birth to her only child. You'll sleep where her husband slept, God rest his long-departed soul."

"Ramon. Where. Did. The. Dear. Departed. Husband. Of. This. Charming. Hostess. Sleep?"

Ramon smiled. (Otis wondered if Ramon ever did not smile.) His companions followed him through a door at the back of the house to a porch. Screened panels enclosed the outdoor room. A rope hammock swung there. Ramon patted it like he would show affection to a prize-winning thoroughbred that had brought a perfecta home to Ramon's pocket.

CHAPTER FIVE

Otis parked the Thunderbird in front of a barn on the edge of town. Much of the structure's paint had been beaten away by years of weather. "This is the place," he said.

El Tigre Azul stepped out of the car. "You sure?"

Otis joined him. "Ramon gave me the name of this place, said to ask anybody where it was. I did. I picked you up, this is where he said to go." Ramon had said, "Go to Ruiz." Otis looked, but no business sign was visible on or around the building.

His companion wasn't so sure about Otis' translation skills. "Why are we here?"

Otis shrugged. "Ramon didn't say. Just said come here." He scratched his chin. "I don't think he likes me much."

The barn doors were open. Flattened cigarette butts littered the crushed gravel near the doorway. Noises rolled out to meet them as they entered the large, open area. A Volkswagen sat inside near the entrance, its engine exposed. Beside it on stationary jacks was a rusting pickup truck. A figure crawled from under the truck. When the man stood up, the travelers saw he was squat but had long, thick-muscled arms. He wore coveralls that were smeared black with grease and oil.

"*Hola*, El Tigre Azul! I saw you fight this morning. You were great!" He wiped one of his paws with a blackened rag and shook hands with the wrestler. "That Rey is trouble. Always has been. Come on in."

The two men followed the mechanic into the shade of the garage. "I'm Ruiz."

Otis wondered if Ruiz was his first or last name.

Ruiz dropped the rag on the hood of the pickup. "You look well rested after the fight."

"Well, yes," El Tigre said. Otis noted a tone of surprise in his voice. Despite The Blue Tiger's misgivings, he had dropped to sleep soon as he'd gotten arranged in the hammock Ramon had shown him. He'd slept soundly until he was prodded from sleep. He had jerked awake to see the little old woman jabbing him with a broomstick. "Okay, okay!" he'd said and waved her away. He stopped himself from asking if she rode that thing at night.

"Good! Good!" Ruiz clapped his hands together. "Let's get you ready for your massage."

"My massage?"

"Yes! Didn't Ramon tell you about the massage?"

El Tigre shook his head.

"My friend, you are very fortunate. You are to experience a massage like you have never had!"

"Ah. Who will be giving it?"

He clapped his hands again. "Ruiz, of course!"

El Tigre Azul and Otis both looked at the mechanic's grimy hands and broken nails.

Ruiz gestured. "There is a shed behind the barn. That's where I give the massage."

They stepped out the back door of the garage. El Tigre saw the shed. Scattered about the weedy lot was a backhoe, a concrete mixing truck, and a bulldozer. All looked as if they had been cannibalized for parts.

A clamor from another barn, about a hundred yards away, reached their ears.

"What's that noise?" Otis asked.

"Omar's cockfights," Ruiz said. "Big crowd up there all the time."


CHAPTER SIX

Omar was sweating and happy. His pockets were full of money. The barn was full of shouting, sweating people whose pockets—in some cases—were full of money or—in other cases—becoming emptier as the afternoon wore on.

The clamor was all focused on the pit. Two cocks hopped and squawked and darted. Feathers swirled into the air with sawdust, then floated slowly to the ground again. Motes of dust climbed the rays of light entering between the barn wall's warped boards.

One of the fighting cocks screeched and a spray of blood spattered half a dozen faces at the front of the crowd. A roar surged within the building: a tone of triumph mixed with the sour note of dismay from the hundred throats of the throng surrounding the pit.

Money changed hands while the losing owner stepped into the pit to retrieve his fallen bird. Omar surveyed the crowd, checked the positions of his workers who moved among the spectators. They kept an eye out for troublemakers, ready to hustle out anyone who made a move to start a fight. Voices might be raised, but regulars to Omar's establishment knew that if they crossed the line, they would quickly find themselves outside the door—most likely with most or all of their winnings taken as a penalty for their bad behavior.

An old man who worked for Omar swept the pit, spread fresh sawdust over the blood spatters and feathers, then raked it out smooth. Soon the next two cocks had begun their fierce battle, and hard shouts rose in volume.

Someone grabbed Omar's shoulder, proposed a fresh side bet. His gaze followed the flashing money, but he heard over the din, "Look at the size of that rooster!"

Feathers flew.

A cock screeched.

The crowd howled.

Omar checked the placement of his muscled lurkers, saw the stunned looks on their faces. He turned toward the pit.

The noise that came from his mouth sounded like a bark.

One fighting cock—the red one, feathers bristling from its skin—was noticeably larger than its opponent: more than twice its size, in fact.

And growing.

While Omar watched—while everyone watched—within half a minute, the larger rooster grew still bigger. In only a few moments it was the size of a large dog.

Omar grabbed the arm of a man beside him. "Whose bird is that?" he hissed.

"Jaime Hernandez," came the answer, then the man pulled away.

Dust flew. The smaller cock hopped and attacked despite the changes to the larger battler. The shouts from the spectators had grown shriller.

Omar pointed. A note of hysteria rattled in his voice: "That chicken is cheating!"

CHAPTER SEVEN

El Tigre Azul was following Ruiz to the shed. His pace was slow. He looked at the mechanic's grimy hands and tried to think of reasons for avoiding a massage. He didn't want to insult the man.

He wanted, instead, to insult Ramon.

Then he stopped. He had caught a faint whiff of something—a smell that he didn't know, but it tweaked at his memory all the same, familiar but unnameable.

Ruiz stopped. Looked at the wrestler.

"What is it?" he asked.

"Do you smell something?"

The mechanic raised his chin, closed his eyes. "Yes."

"What is it?"

"That smell?"

"Yes."

Ruiz shrugged. "*La bruja.*"

"Ah." El Tigre did not know at that moment whether his eyes were open or closed, because what he saw was not Ruiz or the shed. Instead, he saw the lined face of his grandmother, shadow-dappled by the sun falling through the leaves of the tree under which she sat with her grandson.

Her eyes were closed. "Here is what I see," she said. She touched the bark of the tree. She inhaled evenly. "*Arbol del sicomoro.*"

His grandmother was blind.

"You knew that, *Abuelita*," he said. He chuckled. "You come to this tree every day."

"Not every day," she corrected. "But that is what I see. Close your eyes. Now smell the air."

He sniffed, exaggerating like a clown mimicking a dog. He did not notice anything in particular that made him think of the tree.

"Keep your eyes closed. Now smell. Not so hard. Just breathe in and pay attention to your nose."

He giggled at that. "Dirt."

"Very good. Now you are seeing like I see."

He opened his eyes, saw her toss the handful of soil away. "Close those eyes again."

"How did you know?"

"I know little boys."

He closed his eyes.

She held things under his nose and had him identify them. "No guessing. Tell me what your nose sees."

A flower. "Rose." A banana. "Very good."

"My baseball glove."

"You see, you did not look, but you knew what it was."

"I can see with my nose!"

"Your nose may need spectacles, but it is improving."

She chuckled with her husky voice and he giggled.

Then she grabbed him, held him tight.

He was frightened. "*Abuelita*—"

"Hush." She held him close. "Close your eyes."

He did.

"Smell."

He did so.

He inhaled something he couldn't identify. A sour, musky smell; a sweetness of just-turned earth; something bitter. Hot tar, and a chicken three days dead in the road. A tang that snapped at the back of his throat like vinegar.

A curious smell, intriguing, but not so inviting that it didn't leave a sour taste on the mind's tongue.

"What is the mind's tongue?" El Tigre muttered.

Ruiz looked at him. "*Que?*"

His grandmother's arm went around his boy-sized shoulders, cranked him closer to her body. She pressed them both against the trunk of the tree. Her free hand covered his mouth.

"Do not forget that smell," she hissed into his ear. "When you smell it, stay away. Run far, my boy."

He spoke, his lips urging against her palm. "What is it?"

"*La bruja*," she hissed.

"Ah." El Tigre could see Ruiz again. He could hear, finally, the racket from the cockfight barn.

He looked that way.

A mule came charging toward them from the parked cars clustered outside the barn.

With a crackling roar, the building's roof slammed into the sky.


CHAPTER EIGHT

Reynaldo Rey burned with humiliation. His tongue was bitter. The rims of his eyes felt fiery.

He had left the gymnasium without showering. He simply changed clothes and stomped away from the building, avoiding the spectators who crowded at the entrance to see El Tigre Azul.

A block away from the gym he encountered two men playing dominoes. He kicked their table and scattered the ivory squares.

The old men stood and shouted, and Rey shoved them into their chairs and stalked on.

Rey pushed through a peeling door set in the middle of a small building that enclosed darkness and stale cigarette smoke, a bar, and a few men drinking from glasses. Wan light filtered through ragged curtains hung over the two windows.

The bartender had eyes like an owl. He recognized Rey in the dark, and he placed a glass of tequila on the bar. The young wrestler downed the drink, rapped the bartop for a refill.

When he finished, he left without paying. The bartender stared at the closed door for several moments, as though waiting for Rey to return with money.

The door remained closed.

The men who were drinking when Rey entered had moved away from the bar and taken seats at tables. Once Rey left, they drifted back to the bar with their glasses.

Rey continued his furious march past a junkyard with rusting shapes piled in precarious heaps behind a chain link fence. Dogs growled and barked from within the labyrinth. He couldn't see them, but they could smell his anger.

Beyond the junkyard stood a small house. The yard was tidy, and its shrubs and flowering plants were well tended, the structure whitewashed and clean. Flagstones marked a path to the door. Chickens patrolled the vicinity. One red-bristled hog lolled in a dust hole.

Rey advanced. The chickens fussed and scattered. The hog snurfled as Rey passed, then resumed its snoring.

The young man rapped on the door.

A voice called from within: "Come in, Rey."

He entered into a tidy home. The furnishings were simple, but everything was clean and tidy.

A handsome woman approached him from a doorway opposite the entrance. She looked about forty years old, but an air of youth surrounded her. Her black eyes flashed. Above a black skirt she wore a V-neck sweater, dark blue, that revealed a deep cleavage, and her breasts swelled against the sweater's fabric. Rey had seen the ocean, and as he looked at those breasts he thought of sea waves surging to crest and froth. He was unaware that he cupped his hands to catch the sea foam he imagined rolling toward him.

She stood close and took one of his hands in hers. Rey smelled her perfume. He was a bit dizzy.

"Rey, I can feel the anger pulsing in your hands," the woman said. "What is wrong?"

"I need your help."

"Your face is red," she said. "Your throat is pulsing with anger. I feel it." She placed a hand against his chest. "You are so warm. Come with me."

"No, I need your help." Rey looked into her eyes and felt still dizzier.

"I will help you. But come with me now," she insisted. She pulled him—not a tug, but a slow, smooth movement like the current of a river—and he stepped along, flowing through a doorway. He stood there while she closed the door, and then his arms went around her waist when he felt the coolness of her cheek press against his neck.

Outside in the yard the chickens remained unruffled when the woman's voice could be heard: "Rey! REY! Rey—oh, Rey."

The red hog snorted and rolled over.

CHAPTER NINE

Afterwards the woman served Rey coffee at a table in the kitchen. She set the pot on the table, then sat before the man. Her fingers wrapped around a porcelain mug. Rey sipped from his own mug. He looked at the woman. Her eyes seemed to flash with new energy. The flush was gone from his face, but now was visible on hers.

"Do you feel better, Rey?"

"Ana, I . . . am not so boiling hot. But I can't leave this thing with El Tigre Azul as it is."

"The wrestler, hey?" She drank her coffee down in three swift gulps. She closed her eyes, tilted back her head, and spread her hands across her bosom. Rey watched her hands.

"You are very angry," Ana said, "but you must be patient. I will help you. But there is something I must do first."

Rey frowned. He didn't want to hear anything about patience. "What is so important that I have to wait? You are making me wait now."

She looked at him, saw where his gaze was focused, and smiled. "Omar has cheated me."

"Omar?"

"The cockfight man. He cheated me. He must pay."

Rey looked up at her face. Ana smiled again when she saw the confusion tangled in Rey's expression. "Omar doesn't fight chickens. He just runs the place."

"He said I owed money from my bets. He had covered my losses. Antonio Escobedo's little bantam destroyed Orlito Trias' bird yesterday. I won on Antonio's fighter, but Omar took all my winnings. To cover losses, he said." She spat on the floor. Her smile was gone. "He must pay."

The flush that had spread across her face had concentrated at her cheeks. Ana stood. "Put on your shirt. Come with me. Then we will see about your wrestler."

The two walked the path Rey had trod earlier, past the junkyard and its barking dogs and the bar where he didn't pay his bill. In town, they made their way to Omar's barn. A couple of drunks sat on the ground and leaned against a car's fender. They had lost all their money inside the barn and had nothing to use to buy aguardiente. One wearing a red shirt pointed at the pair circling the parked vehicles.

"Why is Rey tagging along with that witch?"

"He follows her like a little puppy."

"Maybe the puppy gets some milk every now and then." The two cackled until the one wearing a yellow shirt started heaving with a rheumy hack.

"It's the wrestling," the other said. "It's no good for Rey. He gets dropped on his head too much."

The two men giggled.

Rey and Ana continued moving around the cars until the woman pointed to a yellow pickup truck.

Two cages sat in the rusty bed of the truck. One was empty. In the other was a bedraggled red bird.

Ana showed her teeth. "That bird belongs to Jaime Hernandez. It doesn't have a chance in hell, and no one will bet anything on it." She gestured to Rey. "Grab it."

The wrestler opened the cage and held the bird as directed. Ana brought up from between her breasts a small leather pouch suspended from a string that hung around her neck. She removed a small bottle and a bulb-ended dropper. She filled the latter with a yellow fluid from the bottle.

With Rey's help, she jabbed the dropper into the red bird's mouth and squeezed the bulb, forcing the liquid down its throat.

Rey returned the fussing bird to its cage. Ana's pouch disappeared back inside her sweater.

They retreated to the edge of the parking area. They watched as Jaime Hernandez later came to get his bird. Rey winced at Ana's strength—she held his hand in one of hers and squeezed while she watched Hernandez return to the barn.

Rey grimaced. "Do you want to go bet on Jaime's bird?"

"No," Ana said, and released her grip on Rey. "I don't need to bet on that fighter. Omar's going to lose more than money today." She plucked at Rey's sleeve. "Let's go find this wrestler."

CHAPTER TEN

Chunks of the roof still rained down. A side of Omar's barn clattered to bits as the giant fighting cock flapped its clipped wings and leaped away from the structure.

Ruiz shook his head. "*Que? Que?*"

The bird hopped and staggered among the cars and trucks parked around what was left of the barn. El Tigre Azul heard screams from the fighting pit. Human screams.

Otis spoke: "It's coming our way."

Ruiz ran into the garage. He rushed out the front door, down the street, out of sight.

"Come on," El Tigre said. He dashed into the garage. Otis followed.

The wrestler snatched up a blackened alternator from a pile of oily rags on the floor. "Get that chain," he directed. He looked over one of the workbenches that lined the walls, scrabbled his fingers through coffee cans and boxes filled with bolts and screws. "Here."

He pushed an eye bolt through a hole in the alternator housing normally used for connecting the alternator to an engine. He tightened the nut, then added a connecting link to attach the new assembly's eye bolt to one end of the chain. The entire length was about forty feet. "Find another chain."

Otis returned to the workbench with another chain. The clatter from outside was growing louder.

"Do this to both ends of your chain," El Tigre said. At the free end of his original chain, the wrestler formed a loop by attaching a connecting link between the chain's last link and another link about a foot and a half back from its end. When he finished, he hefted his chain. "When you're done, bring it out," he told Otis. "And that, too." He pointed to a five-pound sledge hammer. Then he rushed out the back door.

Walking from the garage into the bright afternoon light was like being struck by planes of force. Once El Tigre's eyes adjusted, he saw the vehicles that were tumbled and scattered around the demolished barn. The landscape appeared washed of color by the light, but the giant fighting cock was bright, its colors bold against the sky, each feather's edge sharply outlined. A brown-and-white mutt barked at the approaching bird, scampered backward, turned and barked again. The monster's beak darted down, the dog was gone, just a little cloud of dust left swirling in its place.

The bird was advancing toward the garage. It flapped its clipped wings, apparently furious at what lay spread before it. One horny foot lifted, the monster hopped, the ground vibrated with its landing, then the other foot would rise.

El Tigre began to spin the weighted end of his chain, his hands three feet back from the assembly. As it spun round, he let out more of the chain. Finally about twenty feet of weighted chain swung over his head.

When the cock was within striking distance, the wrestler released the chain. The alternator flew true and struck the chicken's head. The monster flapped, stumbled, fell.

El Tigre turned toward the garage. Otis stood in the door, tossed the five-pound sledge. The wrestler snagged from the air the wheeling handle of the hammer, then rushed to the chicken.

He straddled its neck just as the beast hopped to its feet. He swung the sledge again and again, striking the gigantic bird's neck while he gripped feathers to keep his seat. The cock hopped and flapped, tried to bend its beak around to snatch at the pest trying to hurt it. El Tigre's brain jarred within his skull. His teeth cracked together, his neck felt as though it snapped like a whip. The bird clattered about, and when it slammed to the ground the wrestler's spine seemed to condense and fuse together, then shatter as the bird wheeled again. The monster jumped into the air, spinning, and The Blue Tiger flew off its back. He landed hard, the ground striking across his shoulders. He scrambled up, shook the stars from his head, and dashed away from the darting beak just as it struck the spot on which he'd stood.

He rolled, came to his feet, slammed across the open ground to recover the weighted chain. "Otis! Get the sledge!"

The cock swam on its feet, still dizzied by the blow to its head. El Tigre had time to run the alternator end of his weapon around an arm of the backhoe and through the loop at the chain's other end. He began to swing it again in a widening circle.

The bird rushed the wrestler like a normal chicken after a June bug. El Tigre released the chain. The alternator whipped out, smacked the bird's head again.

The monster swayed, lifted one terrifying foot, then fell over on its side. A dust cloud rose about it.

El Tigre darted forward, snagged the weighted end of the chain, and began to lash it around the giant bird's neck. The creature staggered to its feet before the wrestler could leap free, so he clung to the chain as the cock began to hop and flash about, infuriated to find itself tethered to the backhoe. El Tigre held onto the chain tightly, again being flung about and jarred from head to toe.

"Ho Chi Minh in Paris!"

Even over the bird's clamor, El Tigre Azul heard this shout from the garage. He looked. He tried to focus.

He saw a gorilla.

In a white linen suit.

Wearing penny loafers.

El Tigre Azul squeezed shut his eyes, tried not to bite his tongue while his feathered mount lunged against the chain.

He looked again. The gorilla was gone.

*Must have hit my head harder than I realized,* he thought.

The bird wasn't slowing its efforts. So the wrestler gathered his strength, then leaped free. He struck the ground and rolled away from the cock and into the safety of the garage.

He stood, flexed his limbs to push out the kinks, felt around his mouth with his tongue to check for any bleeding or missing teeth.

Otis patted his shoulder. "You okay?"

Not really able to speak, El Tigre nodded. He gestured for the other chain. Otis handed it over.

Staying out of reach of the cock's beak, El Tigre tied off one end of the second chain to the rusting bulldozer using the loop Otis had fashioned. With the loop at the other end, he pulled through a length of chain to form a lasso, which he started to swing around.

"What are you doing?" Otis asked.

"My great-grandfather was a *charro*," El Tigre answered.

Despite the chain's weight, the spinning loop snaked out, encircled one of the cock's dancing feet, and the wrestler snugged it tight.

Captured, tethered from two directions to heavy anchors, the cock struggled to stay upright. It squawked and flapped and collapsed, fought its way upright, and started its fuss all over.

"*Whew.* That'll work for now," El Tigre said.

The whine of an approaching police vehicle sounded from the front of the garage.

But before the car's occupant could join them, the giant bird burst into flame.

El Tigre and Otis staggered back from the fire. The bird screeched.

A uniformed cop joined the wrestler and Otis. His eyes nearly popped from his skull.

"It's like it was doused with gasoline," Otis said.

Within only a few minutes, nothing remained but a bushel of ashes and a few bones. The chains lay tangled on the scorched ground.

Otis shook his head. "I can hardly believe it."

El Tigre scratched his head. "I've seen some weird stuff the last little bit," he said. He asked Otis, "Did you see a gorilla?"

"Huh?"

"In a suit?"

"What?"

"Never mind."

Otis looked at the ashes. "Smells like fried chicken."

The cop turned to Otis. "I'm hungry."

CHAPTER ELEVEN

The trio walked to Omar's barn. What remained of it.

Overturned and smashed vehicles formed a maze around the edge of the property.

The cop, whose name was Juan, had been ready to leave in a hurry once he heard the explanation of events from El Tigre Azul and Otis. His eyes darted from side to side, looking for more giant troublemakers, but the wrestler convinced him someone with authority needed to investigate the crime scene.

"I'm only a parttime cop," Juan said. "I sell shoes the rest of the time."

Otis shrugged. "So? You're here now."

El Tigre said, "You're the man who escorted me at the fight this morning."

Juan nodded. His Adam's apple jumped.

"You did a good job."

So Juan joined El Tigre and Otis as they stepped through the obstacle course of wrecked cars and trucks.

Juan sucked in his breath when they came across the first body. Close to the shattered barn were several dead gamblers. No wounded folks were present. Apparently anyone who could get away had done so. Everyone else had been killed by the bird or by the collapsing structure.

Otis ran his fingers through his hair. "I count two dozen so far."

The three men continued walking through the site. They came across two men, one in a yellow shirt, the other in a red shirt, bending over one of the bodies and pointing.

"Here now!" Juan jogged over to the pair. "No disturbing the dead!"

Yellow Shirt answered: "We can't disturb the dead. They're dead."

Juan wagged his finger. "You two are drunk!"

"That's probably true," Red Shirt answered. "We can't be very disturbed either. But we're not dead."

Yellow Shirt pointed at the body before them. "Omar."

Juan gasped. "You're right!"

The wrestler and Otis had joined the men. "He owned the barn?"

Juan nodded. "He ran the cock fights."

Yellow Shirt shook his head. "No more, Omar."

Red Shirt sniffed. "No more fight cocking for you, Omar."

"You better take us to the drunk tank, Juan." Yellow Shirt spoke, and his companion nodded agreement.

"Why should you get a free meal?" Juan scoffed. "You two are no worse than usual."

"Yes we are," Yellow Shirt said.

"Yes, sir," Red Shirt said.

"We both saw it," Yellow Shirt said.

"Yes, sir."

"Big."

"Giant."

"Frightening."

"Chicken."

"Killer chicken."

Juan interrupted: "Shut up."

El Tigre added, "We all saw it."

Yellow Shirt and Red Shirt leaned forward, eyed the other three men closely. Yellow Shirt: "Are you drunk, too?"

"No."

Otis noted, "But I could use a cold beer."

Juan shooed the drunks away from the crime scene. "Get out of here. Go home. Or somewhere. Leave us to work."

A crowd had begun to gather. Juan started detailing citizens to certain duties: identifying the dead, arranging transport to the mortuary, looking for survivors.

El Tigre and Otis left him to it. They had given their statements. They were ready to find Ramon.

Who happened to be standing by the smoking ground—all that was left of the giant fighting cock.

"Did you see these chains?" he asked as they approached.

The links were melted, some cooled into a solid length.

"Hot fire," he said.

The wrestler put his hand on Ramon's shoulder. "Ramon, I'm tired. I'm ready to go home."

"You've got another fight tonight!"

Blood trickled from one of El Tigre's nostrils. His clothes were torn, dirty. His elbows were scraped, his bloody knees showed through the holes in his trousers. He said, "I've already fought a mean little octopus and a giant chicken today. I'm wore out."

Ramon shook his head. Vigorously. So vigorously, Otis thought it might be possible for Ramon's hair to fly off his head.

"This will go bad for you if you don't fight tonight. Think of the charity! Think of the *niños*!"

El Tigre's shoulders drooped. He imagined reclining in the chair before the TV in his aunt's house. He imagined what the play of light on the water while snorkeling might look like to his aunt. He considered scuba diving and the weight of an ocean pushing on his shoulders.

"All right," he said. "Let's go."

Otis looked at Ramon and shook his head. "Tsk."

Through the garage—there still was no sign of Ruiz—and out the front door.

The Blue Tiger's Thunderbird jumped into the air in a billowing ball of bright, roiling flame.

The blast knocked the three men to the ground. They staggered to their feet. Dead cigarette butts clung to their clothing.

They watched black smoke rush into the air from the twisted wreck of the car. Otis sobbed, his dream of again driving the road rocket as crushed as the actual vehicle before him.

"Oh man," he said. "That's not cool."

## CHAPTER TWELVE

Ramon got them to the evening's match. A ring was set up outdoors. Lights were arranged to shine on the ring and the wrestlers. The crowd sat in rows of folding chairs surrounding the ring. Everything was in darkness except the fighters.

El Tigre Azul climbed through the ropes. He staggered a little as he stood up. He ached everywhere. Even his toes hurt. And he felt dirty and itchy within his wrestling costume. He wanted to pull his togs off. He pictured a sumo wrestler in his mind—naked but for that big rag knotted around his crotch. That crotch knot might be a bit uncomfortable at first, but being otherwise naked in a fight in the outside heat might feel good, a way to feel any breeze that might manage to get through that assault of Hollywood lighting fixtures.

He blinked against the light, squinted across the ring. He saw his opponent.

Good grief! He rubbed his head. Maybe his brain was damaged during the chicken fight.

He looked again.

The wrestler on the other side of the ring was a gorilla.

A gorilla in wrestling tights and shiny boots.

El Tigre staggered back, made a move to clamber away through the ropes and out of the ring.

"Hey! Hey, come back!"

The gorilla was calling.

El Tigre shook his head, advanced toward his opponent. He put a hand up to shield it against the light.

The gorilla was really a man in a mask. A gorilla mask.

"*Hola*, El Tigre Azul, it's an honor to fight you."

The Blue Tiger squinted. "Who are you?"

"Dr. Zaius." He reached out a hand. El Tigre shook it, not quite sure what else he should do. "Really, Dr. Zaius should be an orangutan, but I could only find a gorilla mask."

"Uh, usually wrestlers have masks that, uh, aren't really masks of animals."

"Oh, I don't mind." The mask seemed to smile. "Can we fight now?"

The official separated the two men. El Tigre trudged back to his corner. He didn't usually hear the crowd when he fought, or even notice them in the moments before a match began. But the shouts and clapping, the whistles and calls all seemed to penetrate the mask on this evening. *I'm very tired*, he thought. *I hope this monkey doesn't bite.*

The bell sounded, the wrestlers met in the center of the ring. They circled, then clinched.

As they grappled, Dr. Zaius said, "I saw you fight that giant chicken today. You were magnificent!"

El Tigre normally didn't chat while he fought, but his surprise shook his concentration. "So I did see you today!"

He flipped the gorilla to the mat.

"Cleopatra's milk bath!" Dr. Zaius exclaimed. The jolt had rattled him. But he was quickly on his feet and on the offensive.

The gorilla had a child-like exuberance for the battle. El Tigre found it refreshing after the bout he'd had that morning with the boorish Reynaldo Rey, and he began to enjoy the match.

The Blue Tiger tossed Dr. Zaius to the floor of the ring, flung his body atop that of the gorilla. "Call you Ishmael!" the latter shouted, then squirmed out from under his opponent.

*Whew*, thought El Tigre, *this could go on all night*. Even though he felt a bit revived by the fun he was having with Dr. Zaius, his long day had taken its toll.

The third round. The spectators were on their feet, cheering wildly.

The wrestlers grappled. Dr. Zaius got a grip on his opponent's waist, swung him to the mat. He whipped around behind El Tigre Azul, pulled him to a sitting position, held him in a chinlock.

The Blue Tiger squeezed Dr. Zaius' forearm with all the strength in his fingers. The gorilla-man groaned, while El Tigre pulled his feet up close to his buttocks, his soles flat on the mat. He pushed back in a sudden surge from his legs, toppling Dr. Zaius and breaking his hold.

Dr. Zaius rolled over on his belly to scramble to his feet, but El Tigre was quick, got astride the gorilla-man's back, then grabbed him with *la de a caballo*. Dr. Zaius was immobilized.

The crowd roared.

Despite his discomfort, Dr. Zaius grinned.

He shrugged and twisted, then El Tigre used Dr. Zaius' momentum to fling the gorilla-man onto his back. He slammed onto the supine combatant, pinned his shoulders to the mat for the three count, then leaped to his feet.

The crowd went wild, screaming, cheering. Dr. Zaius wobbled to his feet, lifted El Tigre's hand high. Folding chairs went flying through the air as the spectators gave in to a sweaty ecstasy.

45

Above the noise, Dr. Zaius shouted, "By the great horn spoon! It is an honor and a pleasure to be defeated by you!"

CHAPTER THIRTEEN

Once the crowd finally scattered, the wrestlers got clean and dressed in fresh clothes. Dr. Zaius supplied El Tigre Azul with a change of clothes, because everything The Blue Tiger and Otis had brought with them was destroyed with the Thunderbird. The gorilla-man's clothing wasn't a perfect fit for El Tigre, but he greatly appreciated the help.

Dr. Zaius drove his honored opponent and Otis to a place to eat and drink. Zaius' vehicle was a decommissioned Army Jeep with no roof or doors. He drove as though he considered the Jeep his road rocket, Otis thought, but Zaius' path was twisty rather than straight, and his passengers clung to their seats with a great fervor. When Zaius finally stopped and killed the engine, Otis whispered to El Tigre, "My fingerprints are permanently embedded in the frame of that seat."

The Blue Tiger replied, "The chicken gave me a safer ride."

Despite the thrills of the ride, Zaius delivered them to a quiet eatery lit by candles. They sat at a table on the patio, and their hostess brought a pitcher of water and a chilled crock of sangria.

"Steaks for everyone!" ordered Dr. Zaius, and he poured drinks for his guests before lifting a cup of his own. "*Mabuhay!*" he toasted.

The meal was excellent. Lulled by food, drink, and the darkness, the three men shared anecdotes and camaraderie warmed by the soft light from the candles.

"Where did you get this name?" El Tigre asked.

The gorilla-man scratched his wide-spread nostrils. "I saw this movie with Charlton Heston: *El Planeta de los Simios*. It changed my life. I realized the world will go spinning along its way with no regard for my hopes and dreams, and I better grab the handles of Fate's bicycle with both hands and a mouth full of zest."

Otis tried to follow this explanation, but he was more fascinated that Zaius could actually drink while wearing that gorilla mask without dribbling all over the table.

"Okay," El Tigre said, "so *The Planet of the Apes*."

"Yes, Dr. Zaius is in the movie. He's an orangutan."

"You mentioned that."

"He's really quite the character. So I adopted his name for my wrestling moniker."

The gorilla-man offered cigars. His guests declined. Otis watched carefully as Zaius lit and puffed the Gran Corona. He was curious how the wrestler managed not to ignite his fur.

Smoke rings puffed out of the mask's nostrils—alternating from one nostril, then the other.

Otis nodded. "That's cool."

Zaius turned toward him. "What brings you to Mexico, Señor Otis?"

The past few years, Otis' inclination was to respond to direct questions by lying earnestly. He seemed to have no control over this response. It just happened. He rarely remembered the words that came out of his mouth.

But his experiences with El Tigre during recent months had brought Otis to a point of mastering this habit. So he answered truthfully: "Love."

"Love?"

"Maybe just romance. But it felt like love." He stared at one of the candles as if the flame would burn an image from his mind. "I met a girl. We fell in love. I thought we fell in love. She said she did, too, when I said so. Then I had to leave town for a week. When I came home, she was gone. People told me she had family here, so I came looking."

"Did you find her?"

Otis shook his head. His sadness seemed to his companions to dim the light from the candles.

"Ho, love is often crueler than hate!"

At this shout, the three men turned to see a new arrival swagger into the light of the patio: another masked wrestler. His thick, black mustache covered most of his face not already hidden by his bronze-colored mask. He was big, with broader shoulders than El Tigre Azul. His hands were big—Otis could imagine this fellow lifting a man off the floor with just one fist clutching a collar.

He plopped down in a chair by their table. Otis wrinkled his nose at the unclean smell that wafted in with the newcomer. He looked as though he had slept in his suit for a week. Well, thought Otis, after today's excitement, I might not look or smell so much better myself.

"*Hola*, Tigre!"

The Blue Tiger responded with less enthusiasm: "*Hola*, El Puño de Bronce."

Dr. Zaius thumped the table. "Antony and Cleopatra! I saw you fight years ago—Omar the One-Eyed Juggernaut. You thoroughly trounced him!"

"He has a blind side," muttered The Blue Tiger.

"I like Omar," the new arrival said. He brushed his mustache with the fingers of one hand. The light from the candles gave a glow to his dark brown skin, darker than the bronze coloring of his mask. "What are we drinking here?" He reached for Dr. Zaius' glass, sniffed the contents. "Hmm. Tequila would be better, but this isn't so bad. Pour me up one of those, sonny."

Dr. Zaius complied with glee.

"*Vida viva*," toasted El Puño de Bronce, and he downed the drink in one gulp. He gestured for another. "This place needs a juke box. I could go for some Jerry Lee Lewis."

El Tigre asked, "What brings you out here to the countryside, El Puño?"

The older fighter smiled. The smile communicated little mirth, but some warmth of affection was evident. "I heard you were here, raising money for orphans. I want to contribute. But," and he pointed, "I heard about the real fight today—no disrespect, Doctor—with the chicken."

"Oh, it was magnificent!" Dr. Zaius could not restrain his enthusiasm.

"You saw it?"

"Oh yes!"

The bronze fighter nodded. "This is a strange business, Tigre."

The Blue Tiger also nodded. El Puño de Bronce was a strange one. At least he was a puzzle to El Tigre. Slovenly in his appearance, nearly drunk everytime he was in public, but carrying the mystique of a great fighter. Showing up to fight nobodies in out-of-the-way places. And this affection he demonstrated toward the younger fighters, of an aging master toward those who followed in his path: El Tigre understood, but he felt uncomfortable about it all the same.

"I agree," El Tigre said. "And my car was bombed immediately after."

"Ho, that's bad. This is more excitement they've seen here since the Glanton gang rode through.[3] Someone doesn't like you."

"That's not a small number," El Tigre admitted.

El Puño de Bronce chuckled. "More's the reason," he said, and raised his glass for a refill.

That's when they heard a clatter in the darkness outside the patio. El Puño de Bronce was on his feet in a second, dashing out into the dark, carrying his chair with him. They heard a yell, then the raucous chatter of an automatic rifle. The forms of two men were silhouetted in the rapid flash from the gun barrel.

"Down!" shouted El Tigre, and the men hit the deck as bullets splintered their table. A lamp shattered, and a tablecloth began to burn.

The shooting ceased. A car door slammed as an engine revved and tires squealed. The three men got to their feet as El Puño de Bronce stepped back into the light. All that remained of the chair was one leg, which he still carried. His other hand held the automatic rifle they'd heard.

He dropped the chair leg, tossed the gun onto their table. He dropped into another chair. "Got away. I tripped in the dark." He grinned, pointed at the chair leg. "I got in a good whack, though."

Otis slapped at the tablecloth, put out the fire. He stared at this big man who moved like a sloth when a drink was in his hand, but could leap like a puma to face a hail of bullets.

One of the candles flared brighter. Sparks flew from the wick.

El Tigre shouted: "A fuse!"

El Puño roared: "Out!

The group ran from the patio. The candle bomb flashed and boomed. The men were slapped from their feet. Splinters of rock and furniture flew like shrapnel.

The wrestlers and Otis staggered to their feet, stumbled around. Each noticed the others talking, but no one could hear anyone else. Shreds of smoke floated about in the dark, lit by a streetlight several yards away.

El Tigre pointed. Otis looked at his arm. Blood ran down its length. He didn't even feel his injury.

He sat on the ground. The Blue Tiger began to clean and tend Otis' wound.

They didn't hear the whine of a police siren. When Juan the Cop approached, the four were sitting on the ground, waiting for their hearing to return. He looked at these men in their tattered, blackened clothes. A sort of dull patience was evident on the faces of three. Juan couldn't make out Dr. Zaius' expression, or what it might mean. Maybe he was patient like the rest. Maybe he was bored.

"Is anyone hurt?" Juan asked. "What are you doing? What happened here?"

El Tigre couldn't hear Juan, but after their encounter that afternoon, he could imagine what the policeman was saying. So he responded: "It was a bomb, Juan. We're resting until we can hear again."

El Puño de Bronce spat. He looked at the hole where the cap of his shoe had been blasted away, and he could see his toes wiggle through the ragged sock on his foot. "I don't know what The Tiger is saying, Cop, but when we can hear each other again, we're gonna go kick some ass."


CHAPTER FOURTEEN

Rey and his buxom paramour, Ana, had witnessed the giant fighting cock's rampage. Ana clutched her throat with one hand, gripped Rey's near elbow with the other. Her bosom heaved as she panted. She released her grip on Rey and pressed a fist to her breast as she fought for air.

"Did you see?" she cried. "Did you see my bird fling Omar into the air? It crushed him with its beak!"

Her face grew flushed as they watched El Tigre Azul battle the cock.

"That's him!" shouted Rey. "Kill him, bird! Kill him!"

Rey sobbed when the creature burst into flame. "No! No!"

"Come along, Rey. Come!" Ana pulled him away from the wreckage and scattered bodies. Her face was bright red and seemed to glow. "Come on." Rey staggered along as the woman tugged his arm. "Come with me."

They passed a small shoe store. Ana turned the corner of the building with Rey in tow. Behind the shoe store was housed a bicycle repair shop. A sign over a wide door was lit by a single large fixture that had been salvaged by the shop owner from a street light. The light was glowing even though dusk wasn't yet near.

"Come, Rey." Ana pulled the young man toward a set of wooden stairs attached to the other side of the building.

"Wait, this is where I live," Rey protested.

"It's closer than home," Ana said.

A sturdy woman stepped out of the repair shop. She wore a grease-stained smock and carried a crescent wrench. Her long gray hair was pulled back in a sort of pony tail, but it bristled out from the restraining band like the tail of a comet. She called out, "Where are you going?"

"Leave us be, Ursula," snapped Ana.

"Rey, you cannot have a woman upstairs."

"Shut up!" Ana made a fist with her free hand and shook it at Ursula.

In turn, Ursula shook her wrench at Ana. "I know you are a *bruja*, but I am not afraid of you. Rey, you know the rules for living here."

The light in the fixture buzzed, went out. The glass globe detached from its metal shroud and fell. The glass broke into halves when it struck Ursula's head. The woman fell like a skull-sledged ox. The wrench clattered with a *ring!* on the ground.

Ana pulled Rey up the stairs. "Come up here," she demanded.

At the top of the steps, she pushed Rey inside the apartment, slammed shut the door.

Minutes later, dogs slunk away from the area when Ana's shouts rang out from the upstairs window.

That evening, the pair entered the bar Rey had visited earlier. When they came in the door, the drinkers at the bar started moving toward the tables. When Ana began to lead Rey to a table, the other patrons returned to the bar.

Ana poured tequila into two glasses. The light in the place was no brighter than it had been in the afternoon, even though it was night-black outside. Despite the dim illumination, Rey could see how vibrant Ana appeared. Her eyes flashed. The thong with its pouch still hung from her neck, disappeared in the valley between her breasts, and his gaze focused on a blush that rose from her cleavage, a fan of pink that raised his desire for her touch. He clutched the sides of the table. He wanted to feel her skin against his palms.

His momentary stupor was broken as Ana thumped the glass before him. "Drink!" she ordered.

He did so. Then he hissed: "El Tigre Azul still lives! Your bird failed!"

"Quiet!" she hissed in return. "The bird killed Omar. That's what I wanted, that's what it did."

"But it blew up."

She waved away the complaint. "Rey, you must understand. A fighting cock, it's a small bird. When it grows so big, it's body doesn't have the ability to sustain that size. Its own body burned itself up! I'm not surprised."

"But what about El Tigre?"

She shushed him.

The light in the bar was so weak, Ana and Rey had not seen three men sitting at a corner table, where the illumination hardly reached at all.

Ana focused her attention on the men and their conversation.

One rested his head on the table. His jaw was purple and swollen.

The others maneuvered their drinks around him. The first still wore his hat and a pair of dark glasses indoors. The second had a glum expression and poured tequila into his mouth direct from a bottle.

"We are supposed to work together." The man wearing the hat said this. He spoke in a monotone, and no expression showed on the part of his face that was visible. "We are the Limbs. We work together. But you didn't tell us about the bomb."

"We are the Arms!" hissed the other man who still sat upright. "El Tigre amputated a Hand!"

The man on the table groaned.

"Shut up!" The man who had identified himself as one of the Arms seemed able to speak only in a hissing manner.

The man in the hat spoke up: "Quiet. This gets us nowhere. He has allies now, and we must plan better if we are to kill him."

"Ah, Rey, you see," whispered Ana, "there are others who will do your bidding. And you don't even have to tell them."

Rey leaned forward. "They are gangsters? Assassins?"

A fourth man entered, joined the three plotters. He told the others, "They are with the policeman. I think they are staying in town. We won't have to track them anywhere else."

Ana smiled. Her eyes narrowed. The more she smiled, the more her eyes disappeared into shadow.

"They may do your work for you, Rey."

"Perhaps." He looked doubtful. The sullen expression had returned to his face, darkening his features, turning his appearance into that of a pouting young boy.

"And if they don't finish the job," Ana continued, "they will at least tire out El Tigre. Then you will sweep in and destroy him, face to face, just as you have dreamed."

Rey sat a bit straighter. He was not entirely cheered, but his mood was not so black as it had been a few minutes ago.

He felt Ana's hand high on his thigh. "We will watch them, Rey. And we will learn from their mistakes with no danger to ourselves."

She stroked his leg. He heard her purr.

Rey felt a heaviness in his diaphragm. A sudden exhaustion settled in his chest, weighed on his shoulders.

## CHAPTER FIFTEEN

The wrestlers were still with Juan the Cop, who stood looking at them. Dark rings circled his eyes. The fighters leaned against the police car. The effects of the blast had dwindled, and their hearing had returned.

Juan looked like a man who was near to being frantic, but was too tired to make it. "I don't know what to do with you. I could throw you in the jail, but someone might blow it up. Then you'd be dead, and we would have no jail."

El Puño de Bronce nodded. "And you might be dead, too."

"I thought of that," Juan said. "Wherever I take you, you're a danger to someone else."

Dr. Zaius thumped the car hood. "Gutenberg and Duesenberg, we're dangers to ourselves!"

"I thought of that, too," Juan said. "All I can figure, you have to leave town."

"You're throwing us out?" Otis asked. He held a hand over the pad covering the wound to his other arm.

"That's what I said."

"We're not going, Cop," El Puño said.

"What?" Juan sputtered a moment, surprised by this rebellion to his authority. "What do you mean?"

El Tigre Azul spoke up: "Whoever is trying to harm us may mean to harm everyone else in your town when they get through with us. If we leave, who will protect you and your town?"

"Well," Juan said, "well, I will."

"Look at us," El Puño said. "Four of us, and two of us spend our lives fighting bad characters. We're pretty beat up right now. You think you can do better all alone?"

Juan chewed his lip.

"Listen, Juan," El Tigre said, "right now, they're just after us. We'll stay here, draw them out."

"Draw them out?"

"Sure. They seem perfectly willing to attack us. So we wait. When they attack, we clobber them. Then we'll leave your town peacefully."

"All in one piece?"

"Absolutely."

Dr. Zaius asked, "They attack? We clobber?"

El Tigre and El Puño de Bronce nodded.

Otis looked at the gorilla. "I'm glad we have a plan now."

Juan shook his head. "I don't know."

El Puño patted Juan on the shoulder. "Sleep on it, Cop."

Otis nodded. "Sleep sounds good."

A big, shiny Ford drove up, parked beside Juan's car. Ramon stepped out.

"El Tigre, you have a softer heart than I ever imagined," El Puño said. "You still let this pipsqueak manage your affairs? Ramon, come here."

Ramon stopped when he saw El Puño de Bronce. The fighter gestured. Ramon was slow to respond, but he finally stepped up to the big man with the mustache. El Puño put his arm around Ramon's shoulders. *The arm*, Ramon thought, *is very heavy*.

"That's a roomy car, Ramon," El Puño said.

Ramon nodded. He couldn't take his gaze from the fighter's face.

"We need rest, Ramon. You're going to get us beds to sleep in. Comfortable beds, you hear? And you're going to drive us in that roomy car."

Ramon nodded again.

"Let's go."

Before Ramon drove away, El Puño called out from his rolled-down window, "See you tomorrow, Cop!"

Juan waved. He leaned against his car. He felt like weeping.


CHAPTER SIXTEEN

The town offered a hotel with three floors. The building had no elevator, so the fighters and Otis climbed the stairs after El Puño de Bronce directed Ramon to leave and to return with plans for a big breakfast the following morning.

They had no luggage to carry, but all four men were tired after the climb—they were exhausted before ascending the stairs—and each collapsed on a bed with few further words.

The sounds of snoring filled each room, masking any other noises that may have been present.

In the morning, Ramon had a "big breakfast," as directed, delivered to the hotel for the men.

Ramon didn't appear for the meal.

Afterwards, Dr. Zaius stood up from the table and said, "Nothing happened last night."

El Tigre said, "Lucky for us. We didn't set up a watch."

El Puño de Bronce patted a napkin to his mouth and mustache. "We must be very confident."

Otis snorted, said, "Or too tired to think straight."

The man in the bronze mask looked out the window. "Now what?"

"We follow our plan." El Tigre Azul spoke to the old man at the register. He was bald, wore a mustache waxed into two stiff longhorn points, and sported red armbands on his shirt sleeves. He nodded vigorously in response to the fighter's questions, and the light flashed from the top of his hairless head.

Dr. Zaius asked, "What's our plan?"

"Just as we said last night," El Tigre answered. He picked up a small table, maneuvered it through the door. "Get some chairs." He placed the table in the street before the hotel.

Otis brought out a straight chair for his friend. "Remind me: What's our plan?"

El Tigre smiled. "They attack. We clobber."

"Sarah Winchester's unending house!" Dr. Zaius exclaimed. "I feel like I'm in *Rio Bravo*. Or *El Dorado*. I don't remember which."

El Puño de Bronce dropped into a chair. "What are you talking about, Doctor?"

"A John Wayne movie. John Wayne and his buddies are under siege in a western town, waiting for the gang of bad guys to attack."

"Ah. Which movie was that? *Rio Bravo* or *El Dorado*?"

"Well, both of them, really."

"Okay. Doctor, you got any more of those cigars?"

"Si." He handed one over to El Puño, then offered to the others, who declined.

The gorilla and the man in bronze lit up. "Now I'm ready to be attacked," El Puño said, and blew out a vast billow of blue smoke, "and to clobber."

El Tigre surveyed their surroundings. Across the street was a shop with flowers and clay pots and hanging baskets. The man running the shop had one large shutter of boards hinged at the bottom, which he let down from its latch at the top. The shutter dropped down and hung from chains at its corners, forming a sort of bar or tabletop for displaying his wares. There was no window glass in the uncovered opening into his store. He stood inside and faced over the shutter like a barkeeper awaiting customers.

Beside the hotel on the left was a tailor. Its door and shutters remained closed. To the right of the hotel was a *funeraria*. The mortician stepped out his door. He was dressed in black from head to toe. He looked at the men sitting in the street around a small table, nodded, smiled, rubbed his hands together, and disappeared inside his business.

El Tigre chuckled. "Maybe this is a western." He looked at El Puño. "Do you feel like John Wayne?"

The man in bronze tapped ash from his Gran Corona. "I feel more like Gabby Hayes."

Otis looked around. "What do we do now?"

El Tigre answered. "We keep doing what we're doing."

El Puño nodded. "We follow the plan."

Juan the Cop drove up, stopped the car beside their table. His movements were stiff as he stepped from the vehicle. His uniform was wrinkled. The circles around his eyes were coal black.

Otis asked, "Did you sleep in your car last night?"

Juan snapped back, "That is no concern of yours!"

El Puño nodded. "The jail probably isn't safe."

"What are you doing here?" Juan demanded.

The four seated men looked at one another, then at Juan.

"We're following our plan, Cop," answered El Puño.

"What?"

El Tigre nodded. "They attack. We clobber."

"What?"

Dr. Zaius stood. "Do you want to join us? I can get you a chair."

"What? Sit down!" Juan stomped. "I mean—you can't stay here! It's the middle of the street!"

"You said anywhere we go would be in danger," El Tigre said. "Out here, everyone can see us, can stay away and be safe. Look, no one is in the street but us and you."

Juan looked around. The man in the flower store ducked out of sight. The cop looked back at El Tigre.

"Come on, Juan. It'll be all right."

Juan stomped again. But he didn't open his mouth, because he didn't know what to say.


CHAPTER SEVENTEEN

Two drunks were walking in the morning light from the direction of what had once been the scene for Omar's cockfights. One wore a yellow shirt, the other a red shirt. The one in red walked alongside a bicycle. The frame was bent. The back tire was missing, and the rim was a little dinged.

Yellow Shirt said, "You sure Ursula will pay us for this bike?"

"Sure, she likes *bicicletas*."

"Ursula knows us. She knows we don't own a bike."

"We own one now."

"You stole it."

"I never! It was on the ground. It belonged to Hector. A dead man can't own anything."

"You didn't buy it. That's like stealing."

"Who would steal a beat-up bike like this? No one. So no one will suppose we stole it. And it's not worth buying, so no one would want to steal it, or think about stealing it, so why would we steal it?"

"Why will Ursula give us any money for it?"

"I told you she likes *bicicletas*. She'll buy it."

"No, she won't."

They had arrived at the bicycle repair shop. Ursula lay on the ground. A dried worm of blood curled away from her skull in the shape of an elongated S. The halves of the broken light globe lay nearby.

Red Shirt sobbed. "*Amigo*, I am tired of dead people."

Yellow Shirt nodded. "This is bad." He looked up at the window of the next floor. "Do you think Rey knows?"

They left the broken bike beside Ursula's body. Upstairs, Yellow Shirt rapped on the door. It swung open, unlatched. Red Shirt called, "Rey?"

Yellow Shirt wrinkled his nose. "Smell that? That *bruja* has been here."

"Peeyoo."

"I bet she did it."

"What?"

"Killed Ursula."

"That *bruja*, she's bad."

"Crazy Rey."

"Tsk, tsk."

They retrieved the bike after covering Ursula with a blanket from upstairs. Then the two drunks went in search of Juan the Cop.

61

CHAPTER EIGHTEEN

Yellow Shirt and Red Shirt rolled the bicycle along the street until they reached the group in front of the hotel. Red Shirt leaned the bike against the fender of Juan's car.

"Hey, don't scratch the paint. That's an official vehicle."

Yellow Shirt spoke: "Officer Juan, we looked for you all over."

Red Shirt: "The jail."

"Your sister's house."

"Antonio's Bar."

"No one has seen you."

Red Shirt looked at Juan from head to toe. "Did you sleep in your car?"

Juan stomped. "What do you want?"

The two drunks answered in unison: "Ursula's dead."

"What?"

Yellow Shirt nodded. "We think *la bruja* did it."

Red Shirt agreed. "Ursula didn't like *la bruja*."

"She wouldn't let *la bruja* in Rey's apartment."

"Against the rules. We know the rules. We heard Ursula yell 'em at Rey last week."

"But *la bruja* has been in Rey's apartment."

"And Ursula is dead."

"Wait a minute!" Juan protested. "What *bruja*?"

"The one Rey hangs around with," Yellow Shirt said. "Everybody knows. Don't you?"

"Nobody can find him in his car to tell him." Red Shirt snickered.

"Shut up!" Juan shook his finger at Yellow Shirt. "What are you talking about?"

"*La bruja* is bad. She made that chicken get big and kill people at Omar's barn."

"What?"

"Poor Rey. Dropped on his head."

Juan stomped. "Shut up about Rey! Why didn't you tell me about this chicken and the *bruja* yesterday?"

"I don't know," Yellow Shirt said.

Red Shirt raised his hand. "I know. We were drunk. We saw a giant chicken."

"And?" Juan prompted.

"I don't know. I saw a giant chicken. When I see a giant chicken, I've had too much to drink."

Juan swore. "You two! Go tell the mortician about Ursula. I'll go over there and investigate." He opened the car door. "And take this bike with you!" Juan turned toward the men at the table. "And you—don't you go anywhere until I get back."

El Puño nodded. "We're not going anywhere."

El Tigre waved as the car did a three-point turn and wheeled away, chased by dust. "We're following the plan."


CHAPTER NINETEEN

The bald man working the hotel register had brought out a tray to the table in the street. He poured coffee for each of the four men, left the pot behind.

El Tigre raised his cup. "*Gracias.*"

Earlier the hotel man had brought out a metal stand, like a flag stand, placed it beside the table. He went back inside the hotel, returned a few minutes later with a large umbrella. He placed the end in the stand, raised the metal ribs with the fabric vanes attached, and locked in place the large clip that circled the pole. The shade brought a nice relief from the sun and heat.

The fighters had been sitting in the street nearly three hours. No one had come along except Juan and the two drunks. Juan hadn't returned from investigating Ursula's bicycle repair shop. The two drunks had come back out to the street after reporting Ursula's death to the mortician. They sat by the door, their backs against the building housing the *funeraria*.

El Puño de Bronce called over, "You should get off the street. If the action starts hopping, you could get hurt."

Yellow Shirt waved. Red Shirt called out, "Hey, do you want to buy a bicycle?"

El Tigre turned to Otis. "How's your arm?"

"Hurts, but it's okay. Thanks."

"You should stay in Ohio," the man in bronze said. "Safer there."

Someone came around the building, walked in the middle of the street to the table.

"Who's this?" El Puño wondered.

It was clear from the person's form she was a girl. El Tigre squinted against the light. As she approached, her features came clearer. She looked familiar.

She stopped beside the table.

El Tigre stood. So did Otis and Dr. Zaius. El Puño sipped his coffee, watched the girl over the rim of his cup.

The Blue Tiger finally recognized the girl. She was the delicately curved young woman who had smiled at Ramon while he was selling photographs outside yesterday morning's fight with Rey.

"I remember you," El Tigre said. "Outside the gymnasium yesterday. Can we help you?"

"Someone is trying to hurt you," she said.

"You could get hurt just standing here," the man in bronze said. He stared at her while he lit another of the cigars Dr. Zaius had handed out.

She looked at the big fighter in his chair, blue smoke surrounding his head like a storm cloud building around a mountaintop. She returned her attention to El Tigre. "My name is Carmel. I live here. I saw how you fought to help the orphans and the hospital. There are bad people here. I don't want to see you hurt."

She noticed Otis and his bandaged arm. "Look," she said, "already one of you is hurt." Carmel stepped over to him, touched his arm. "You others are fighters—you face evil every day. But this man, he is your friend, and he is truly brave. He fights evil beside you because you are his friends. He is braver than you, for that. But you are foolish to let him stand with you, to be harmed."

El Puño snorted. "Chiquita, I think you are here to help hurt us. You are in league with those evil people who have been trying to kill us, no?"

Carmel stomped her foot. Her eyes flashed. "No! I told you—"

Otis patted her hand where it rested on his arm. A blush had crossed his face while she had spoken of him a few moments ago. The image of the girl was locked into his memory: Her long black hair and dark eyes, the sweet flare of her cheekbones; a slender neck rising from a red sleeveless blouse; a short black skirt; the lovely turnings of her legs. Now he scowled at the man in bronze. "Carmel, we thank you for your concern. But it is dangerous here. You should go home."

She looked up at him. "What is your name?"

He looked surprised, a bit frightened. "Otis."

"Señor Otis, you are a true man among these . . . men." She kissed his cheek with a quick dart of her head, then turned and walked away, returning around the corner of the *funeraria.*

El Puño puffed his cigar. "What was that about?"

No one answered. The others returned to their seats.

"I think she's a vampire," the man in bronze continued. "Have you fought a vampire lately?"

El Tigre frowned. "No."

"Then you're due."

Otis asked, "Was Dean Martin in *Rio Lobo*?"

"No, no," Dr. Zaius said, "different movie. *Rio Bravo*."

El Tigre asks, "Does he sing?"

"Dean Martin? In the movie?"

"Yes."

The gorilla mask made some ludicrous expressions while Dr. Zaius considered. "I guess so. Why would you have Dean Martin in a western if he didn't sing?"

El Tigre nodded. "Be worth watching if Dean Martin sings."

A noise came from one end of the street, then from the other. Before them a big green Dodge pulled into view and idled. Behind them, from the other end of the street, another big car—a yellow Chevrolet—pulled up and paused.

El Puño stood, lay his cigar on the chair seat so the ash end hung over the edge. He nodded toward the Dodge, "There's the rock," and then to the Chevy, "there's the hard place."

The street was a broad thoroughfare. It offered plenty of room for traffic, which had been entirely absent this day. The fighters' table sat in the middle, where there would have been plenty of room for a dividing median, if this were a boulevard.

The drivers of both cars revved their vehicles' engines. The autos roared and bore down on the table, tires screeching and throwing up dust clouds.

El Tigre stood. "Here we go."

El Puño spoke to Otis and Dr. Zaius: "You boys be ready to duck and cover."

The two cars rushed past, one on each side of the table, the driver's side of each car flashing closest to the men in the street. Bits of gravel and dirt were flung into the faces of the fighters.

The Dodge and Chevy wheeled in tight turns, again faced the table. The cars had exchanged places at the ends of the street. The engines roared, the drivers engaged the clutches, the cars rushed forward. They performed the same pass as their first move down the street, wheeled tight squealing U-turns at the ends of the street to again face the table, back in their original positions.

"That *hombre* I whacked last night is driving the Dodge," said El Puño de Bronce. "He doesn't look very happy."

The engines revved again.

El Tigre glanced at the man in bronze. "Ready to dance?"

El Puño looked down at his toes sticking out the hole in his shoes. "*Las cebollas fritas* owe me a pair of dancing shoes."

The cars rushed forward.

El Puño kicked over the table.

"Get down!" El Tigre shouted.

Otis and Dr. Zaius dove for the ground. They attempted to use the table as cover.

On the passenger side of each car, the window had been rolled down. One of the Limbs—an Arm in the Dodge, a Leg in the Chevrolet—reared through the open window of each car, armed with a chattering Thompson submachine gun pointed at the men in the center of the street. The flash of the powder flared as bullets chewed lines advancing from the path of the autos to the table.

Both El Tigre and El Puño leaped, somersaulted like synchronized swimmers of the air. The bullets blew shrapnel from the pavement, ricocheted, shattered a window in the hotel. The firing ceased as the cars came abreast of the table, passed.

The fighters landed on their feet, spun to face the cars. The wheeled juggernauts squealed in tight turns at the ends of the street, throwing up clouds of grit.

El Tigre glanced down. "Okay?"

"Otis is hurt again," Dr. Zaius said. "Other arm. Bullet. Splinter from the table caught him in the jaw."

"I'll, I'll be okay."

El Tigre checked the position of the cars. "He needs a doctor."

El Puño gritted his teeth. "No juke box. No Jerry Lee Lewis. No Los Dug Dug's. I'm tired of dancing."

The cars came on. This time they had traded sides of the street, so the shooters wouldn't have to stop firing, and they would catch the luchadores in a crossfire as they passed.

The man in bronze snatched the umbrella from its stand, collapsed the fabric vanes to form a sort of spear.

El Tigre sprinted toward the onrushing Chevy, the bullets flying past before the sound of their passage touched his ears.

El Puño ran toward the Dodge. He faced the shooter, squinted against the gunpowder flash from the submachine gun. Bullets shredded the fabric of the umbrella and of his already-ragged clothing.

El Tigre leaped. The gunman tried to track him with his path of fire as the fighter arced into the air.

El Puño hefted the umbrella by the shaft like a vaulter carries his pole.

He jumped.

El Tigre came down.

He landed, feet first on the hood of the Chevy.

The metal buckled. The engine broke loose from its moorings, hit the ground.

The feet of El Puño de Bronce bicycled as he sailed through the air.

The point of the umbrella shattered the Dodge's windshield. It skewered the driver, crushing through his sternum, breaking ribs, puncturing a lung, fracturing his spine, pinning him like a bug to the upholstery of the seat.

After El Tigre hit the Chevy hood, he pounced into the air as the car reared upward on its nose. The driver flew through the windshield, flaying the flesh from his face, shredding the coat and shirt from his torso as shards of glass whirled in a glittering cloud about his body, until they all thumped to the ground ahead of the vehicle. El Tigre landed behind the car on his feet, like a cat.

The Chevy's shooter was flung from the passenger window when the car's rear rose from the ground. He still clutched the Thompson, and his finger continued to tug the trigger as he pinwheeled. He didn't hear his own screaming as he spun through the air, didn't hear the stuttering roar of the gun, saw only the flashes from its barrel as time slowed in an adrenaline rush that ended with a snap when he struck the street, cracked his skull, broke his neck.

The legs of the Dodge's impaled driver stiffened when the umbrella point punctured his chest. His feet stomped the brake pedal. The car squealed to a stop.

El Puño gripped the umbrella shaft, twisted, somersaulted over the automobile like a pole vaulter.

On the Dodge's passenger side, the gunman's legs were shattered as he was thrown against the door frame, tossed out the window and onward along the path the Dodge had been traveling. The machine gun went spinning like a lost car tire along the street. The shooter whirled through the air, then struck and rolled along the pavement like a flung doll. When he hit the street, the pavement shattered the bones of his face, then his arms, his pelvis, his spine.

The Chevy fell back onto its four wheels. Dead.

The Dodge's engine growled, sputtered, then died.

The two fighters knocked dust from their tattered clothes, came back to the overturned table. Any exposed flesh of both men carried hundreds of tiny lacerations from exploding glass and tiny bits of bullet lead that broke apart during the projectiles' rush from the barrels of the guns. Their skin appeared wrapped in a net of tiny red threads.

El Puño staggered a bit, picked up his cigar from where it lay, undisturbed, on the chair. After a couple of puffs, a cloud of blue enveloped his head.

"Ah."

El Tigre kneeled by Otis. Dr. Zaius remained untouched.

"Go to the hotel," El Tigre instructed. "Send for a doctor."

The gorilla hustled off.

At El Tigre's request, the man in bronze handed over his shredded jacket. El Tigre tried to hold off the effects of shock by using the folded coat to elevate Otis' legs. He lay the remains of his own jacket over Otis to warm his friend.

He turned when El Puño asked, "Who is this?"

From around the corner of the *funeraria* walked two figures.

"That's Reynaldo Rey," El Tigre said. "Bad boy I wrestled yesterday."

Rey swaggered, chest thrown out, sneer on his lips.

"Who's the other?"

Beside the young man walked an old woman. Her hair was long, wiry, and wild. Her toothless grin added deep creases to her wrinkled face, and one eye rolled in different directions, independent of the other, which gazed with a terrible black light. Her legs were thin, bowed, and blue with thick veins. She wore a tattered black skirt and a thin blue sweater that barely contained her massive, pendulous breasts that swung below her belly. The sweater's V neck was far too revealing, El Puño thought.

Rey looked at Ana when she grabbed his elbow. Her black eyes flashed. He saw the rapid rise and fall of her firm, upthrust breasts as she began to pant with excitement. "You will destroy them, my Rey," she said, and he felt the moist warmth of her mouth as she kissed his neck.

El Tigre sniffed the air.

A sour musk. Overripe fruit. Leaf rot.

"*La bruja*," he said.

El Puño sighed, tapped the ash from his cigar. "I hate witches."

CHAPTER TWENTY

The two drunks remained seated against the wall of the *funeraria*. Red Shirt called out, "Rey, that witch will only get you in trouble. She killed Ursula!"

Rey ignored Red Shirt. His gaze was on El Tigre only.

"Count your breaths, El Tigre!" Rey stamped his foot as he yelled. "They grow fewer in number! Today you will take your last!"

Red Shirt shook his head. "What is Rey talking about?" He nudged his companion with his elbow. "He's going to get his butt kicked."

He giggled. When Yellow Shirt didn't respond, Red Shirt looked at his friend.

Crimson covered the front of the yellow shirt. Two ragged holes in the fabric were clotted with blood.

"Oh, *mi amigo*," Red Shirt sobbed. "*Mi amigo, mi amigo.*"

CHAPTER TWENTY-ONE

El Puño de Bronce dropped the cigar butt, pressed it into the surface of the street with the sole of his blown-out shoe. "Are we still following the plan?"

El Tigre stood beside Otis. "We are."

He looked around. "Where is Juan?"

The man in bronze put his arms akimbo. "That cop is following his own plan. Away from here."

El Tigre called out, "Rey, come sit down. Cool off. Let's have a drink and talk."

In reply, Rey roared.

Then he flashed forward. He rushed them so quickly he bowled over El Puño before the dust rose from where his feet had touched the street. Rey was fast as a speeding car.

The man in bronze was down, and Rey pummeled him. Rapidly. El Tigre could barely see Rey's fists and arms pumping, swinging.

El Puño could neither grunt nor groan before Rey landed another punch, then another and another. Taken by surprise, he was being beaten to death before he could lift an arm in defense.

El Tigre, shocked, realized the witch had enhanced Rey's abilities in some fashion. He rushed to help his friend.

Despite his agony, rage swept through El Puño. No punk is going to kill me with his fists, he thought. He lashed out with his feet. His shoe heels cracked against Rey's shin with a mule's strength, and the young man staggered away.

El Tigre attacked. He was on Rey, swinging him around to get him dizzy, then he punched his face three times. Blood flew from Rey's nose.

The Blue Tiger grabbed Rey in a hammerlock, heaved with all his weight, brought him down to the ground.

Rey shuddered like an engine tearing loose from its mounts. He screeched.

El Tigre tumbled away from him, unable to maintain his hold. Rey was on him, kicking, punching, thumping with his feet, fists, forearms.

He pulled the masked fighter to his feet. The two grappled. El Tigre worked to slip free, but Rey's holds kept shifting and flowing from side to side. He kept El Tigre off balance. The Blue Tiger was reminded again of fighting Rey the other morning, so like the octopus the kid had drawn in the poster.

Then he felt the suckers.

Rey had grown more arms. Arms without bones. His arms had all changed to tentacles, growing from his shoulders like some monster from the black depths of the ocean. Rey's head had swelled, lost its human shape. He was a sea monster on human legs. El Tigre felt he was being torn apart.

He couldn't wrestle those suckered tentacles. Both fighters were shirtless now, the tatters lying in the dust of the street. El Tigre's flesh was marked by the suckers. Blood smeared his skin. He got a little space between him and Rey, pounded the creature's face and chest, sledging blows that would have dropped a man twice Rey's mass.

But the monster's flesh seemed merely to absorb the energy of El Tigre's blows. The tentacles swirled, caught up El Tigre like a doll.

He began to gasp—he was being crushed. El Tigre could feel his ribs grind together.

He dug his fingers into the tentacles, felt the unyielding sinew there, tried to pull and tear away the inhuman flesh.

El Tigre had no breath left even to cry out.

Then Rey flung him across the street with the force of a cannon.

El Tigre flew through the open display window of the flower shop. He crashed into pots, overturned shelves and racks with hoses and bags of soils and plant food. He tumbled and finally stopped, stretched across a bag of fertilizer.

His chest heaved for air.

Tracks of blood like red worms slicked his skin. His internal organs felt like wrung-out dishrags.

He raised his head. Tears smeared his vision, but he made out a figure: The shop owner cowered in a corner, hunkered behind a large urn.

El Tigre got out a whisper: "Stay there."

He rolled off the bag onto his hands and knees. He looked around. He could hear Rey approaching from the street. The monster-that-had-been-Rey screamed out incoherent syllables. But El Tigre could make out the rage powering those exclamations, whatever they were.

El Tigre tamped down his anger. The thought *He's going to kill me* flitted momentarily, but he felt no fear. He continued to search his surroundings.

"Ah."

El Tigre tried to stand, faltered, fell back to his knees. He crawled to a scattering of red bags, each about ten kilos. The labels on each read *Tierra de diatomeas.*

Diatomaceous earth.

He pulled two bags to him.

Rey kicked in the door.

El Tigre used his fingers, tore a hole in the center of each bag.

Rey screamed again. A roaring scream—its volume left a deafened silence in El Tigre's ears.

El Tigre clutched one bag in each hand.

He started to stagger to his feet, then the tentacles snatched him from the floor. He was held suspended in air.

He couldn't get leverage to defend or attack this way.

El Tigre swung the toe of his shoe into Rey's crotch.

The monster bellowed.

It bent at the waist. El Tigre's feet hit the floor.

He moved in closer. The tentacles tightened about his torso.

El Tigre began to swing the bags, wearing them like boxing gloves.

He punched, pounded, clobbered. Rey screeched. Clouds of white dust spewed from the bags as El Tigre slammed them against Rey's head, chest, tentacles. His fists thumped Rey. The white powder from the bags clung to Rey's inhuman skin, swirled in the air like a white storm cloud.

The Rey Monster made a noise—a yowling howl like nothing on earth El Tigre had ever heard. The tentacles tightened, then released El Tigre as Rey ran away, howling his agony.

El Tigre watched Rey's retreat for a few moments. He dropped the emptied red bags.

He fell back, sat hard on a stack of bags containing potting soil.

He lay back as though he reclined in the finest upholstered chair in Mexico.

El Tigre closed his eyes and blew a long, slow breath.

"Hoo."


CHAPTER TWENTY-TWO

In the street, El Puño finally clambered up onto his hands and knees. He had heard the fight in the flower shop, now heard the unholy noise Rey made as his monster form dashed away.

He heard the witch calling after Rey.

The man in bronze had blood caking in his mustache, running across his chin. He spat out a tooth.

His ribs, his shoulders—everything—felt afire.

He pushed up, got to his feet.

He squinted. The street and its buildings swam in his vision, slowed, steadied. The witch was still at the end of the street, facing away toward wherever Rey had run off.

"All right, *bruja*," El Puño called, "your boyfriend is gone. Time to dance with the fellow who steps on everybody's toes."

He took a step. Another. He staggered. Then with each step, his gait strengthened, his stride became more regular.

Ana turned. She looked at him with one fiery black eye and that rolling eye.

She hissed like a viper.

El Puño kept coming.

On the move, without breaking his stride, he snatched up from the street a hubcap from the Dodge. He sailed it like a Frisbee.

The bruja raised her arm. The hubcap slammed into her shoulder, sliced away the sleeve of her sweater, but the old woman appeared unfazed by the blow.

El Puño grinned. "Tough as jerky," he said. "This will be fun."

She flippered her hands at him. He squinted, heard a rush of air approaching from behind.

El Puño ducked.

A bumper from one of the cars wheeled through the air over his head.

He would have been decapitated had he not moved quickly.

"I'm not some punk like Rey," he yelled to her. "We're going to dance, and I'm going to stomp your feet."

He stalked forward.

Ana spun around, kicked up some dust that whipped away along the street.

El Puño stepped over the twisted chrome bumper that had hurtled over his head.

*La bruja* dashed toward the *funeraria*, threw open the door and disappeared inside.

The man in bronze began to trot toward the *funeraria*. He grimaced as pains shot through his body. "You're fast for a bow-legged, evil old cow."

He ignored Red Shirt sobbing beside the doorway.

As he reached for the door handle, El Puño heard a scraping sound, rushing toward the door from its other side.

He stepped away.

A *Crash!* shattered the door to shards as a casket slammed through like a battering ram, landed in the street. El Puño staggered aside just ahead of the pile-driving box as it rattled to pieces. He craned his neck, peered into the darkness of the building, then jumped in through the door.

## CHAPTER TWENTY-THREE

El Tigre Azul rolled off the bags of potting soil. He got to his feet in slow, gradual movements.

He blinked tears from his eyes.

The shop owner still cowered behind an urn.

"You can get up now," El Tigre said. "It's okay."

The man hustled away.

El Tigre staggered from the shop in time to see El Puño de Bronce dash into the *funeraria*.

"That can't be good."

He walked like a man who hadn't moved in three months. He made little grunts and groans as he walked, then began to trot, completely unaware that he uttered any noise at all. He was acutely aware of the sharp knives that seemed to be slicing his skin, his muscles, with each move he made.

He saw the spatters of blood and the lost tooth by the table.

El Tigre turned just long enough to see a young man with a doctor's bag approaching, riding a bicycle. A glance downward showed him Otis peering up through half-closed eyes. He smiled—or grimaced—and offered a half-hearted wave.

El Tigre moved along the street and paused beside the shattered casket outside the *funeraria*. He gazed at the dead man in the yellow shirt. He patted Red Shirt on the shoulder.

Then El Tigre stepped into the *funeraria*.

The witch stood at the opposite end of the room on a sort of dais.

El Puño de Bronce attempted to approach her, but dozens of caskets scooted across the floor to block his progress, apparently shifted by some giant, invisible hand, like massive dominoes scattered across a table top.

*La bruja* stood behind a casket on the raised floor, her hands atop its closed lid. One eye rolled. The other blazed with a fierce light.

A second figure joined her.

It seemed to rise up from the floor, behind the shielding coffin, as from a trapdoor in a theatre stage.

It was a horror.

What may once have been flesh now stretched itself tightly across an eyeless skull like a mummified caul. Its teeth were long, yellow, and recalled the fangs of an ape.

Smoke or mist wrapped its figure like a cape or cloak that flitted, hiding then revealing rancid organs that hung below its rib cage, dripping a thick, yellow liquid.

The horror embraced Ana, kissed her forehead with its lipless mouth.

The witch screamed.

El Tigre whispered, "What is that thing?"

El Puño, dodging the continually moving caskets, yelled out, "I know that bastard!"

He began to curse. He swore a blue streak. He swore like a man who had just invented swearing and exuberantly broadcast his discovery to the world. He swore in languages El Tigre had never heard. Had they heard it, navies from three continents would have blushed.

El Puño snatched up an old candelabra, hurled it at the creature.

The brass object whirled through the horror as though its form were a projection on the smoke. Even the mist that cloaked it remained undisturbed as the candelabra banged against the back wall, fell to the floor.

The caskets continued their thwarting dance, intercepting El Puño's path to the dais, blocking his moves to one or another side. He was being hemmed into a corner.

El Tigre saw all this from the door. He stepped forward, and the pains reawakened in his limbs and torso as he moved. He saw the two figures on the other side of the room, then watched the drifting caskets. He took another step into the room, ready to vault atop the nearest coffin, so he could jump from one to the other to reach the witch and the horror.

El Tigre prepared to launch himself forward. He stopped—two sharp jabs in his ribs shot pains to his spine and abdomen. His reflexes kicked in—El Tigre whirled, right arm extended to sweep his attacker off his feet. His arm stopped, halted when it struck an immovable object: electric pains thrummed from his fingers to his shoulder and neck.

Arm suspended, he turned his head.

A rod. No, a broomstick.

A broomstick had stopped his swinging arm.

El Tigre looked down.

The broomstick was held by the old woman in whose hammock he had napped the previous day.

She wasn't even five feet tall, but she had stopped the force of his blow with no visible effort.

El Tigre looked at those black-marble eyes in her face like a deflated balloon.

"Let her go," the old woman said. "She belongs with him. She doesn't belong here anymore."

El Tigre had heard her speak very clearly, even against the racket made by the ever-shifting caskets scooting across the floor, as if she were talking to him inside a silent church. He glanced again at the horror.

"What is that?" he asked.

"Mictlantecuhtli," she answered, "lord of the underworld."

"Ugh."

The horror opened its mouth.

Then the jawbone unhinged, so its hideous maw opened even wider.

A flood poured out.

Black, viscous fluid gushed from between its teeth, a cataract of foulness that struck the caskets, the floor, knocking over every object in its path. The flood reeked of death: the hundreds and thousands sacrificed to the gods and killed in battle for the glory of the Aztec empire.

Mictlantecuhtli stood unmoving, still clasping Ana, still disgorging the foul-smelling flow. In seconds the room was filled. The caskets and furnishings were picked up from the floor. El Puño and El Tigre lost their footing. All were pushed by the swelling flood toward the wrecked door.

Everything in the room heaved out the small doorway on the crest of a vile wave that struck the pavement, spread, and kept flowing from the *funeraria* entrance. El Tigre rolled into the middle of the street. He sputtered, slapped his hands across his face to clear away the filth. His ears hummed from the wings of a million flies. The coffins piled up inside the *funeraria* doorway, jammed, then shattered into shards against the increasing pressure of the flood. Wood flew out into the street. Then El Puño appeared in a rush of frothy liquid. He was spilled onto the pavement beside El Tigre.

The flood subsided, then melted into the street.

Within two minutes, there was no sign of the foulness that had blasted them out of the *funeraria* and into the street. Only the two fighters and the shattered furnishings remained scattered before the open doorway. The buzz of flies zippered the air, but none were to be seen.

Red Shirt still sobbed, hugging his dead friend. He was oblivious to everything that had just happened.

"Oh man," El Tigre said.

He and El Puño helped each other to their feet.

They hobbled to the *funeraria*, peered inside.

The place was empty. *La bruja* and Mictlantecuhtli were gone. No sign of the black flood remained. Not even its smell.

The little old woman was nowhere in sight. Nor was her broom.

El Tigre touched his sore ribs. His arm still stung where it had hit the broomstick. He groaned, sat down beside Red Shirt.

"Did we follow the plan?" he asked.

El Puño spat, stared at the wet spot beside his foot. "They attacked. We clobbered. Sort of."

"I guess so."

"Hm."

El Tigre sighed. "Give me a giant chicken to fight any day," he said.

CHAPTER TWENTY-FOUR

El Puño finally joined Dr. Zaius, who stood near Otis, still lying in the street.

"What's going on here?" El Tigre asked.

The doctor and the hotel clerk stood near the hotel door.

The girl who had approached them earlier, Carmel, kneeled beside Otis and cooed into his ear.

The gorilla-man shrugged. "She showed up, ran off the doctor. Said she'd look after Otis."

"How is he?"

Dr. Zaius looked over at Otis, saw a smile on his face. "Better, now."

Juan drove up in his police car, got out and shook his fist at the two fighters who stood in tatters, smeared with blood seeping from cuts and wounds. "You two have caused enough trouble. Get out of town! I mean it!"

El Puño laughed. No mirth rode the sound he made. "I can't wait, Cop. But I need some clothes."

Juan opened his mouth. "I—I will buy you clothes. Just get out." He looked surprised at the very words he had spoken.

"Very well." El Puño's smile, barely noticeable beneath his moustache, was grim.

Dr. Zaius asked, "Flo Ziegfeld's pantaloons, what did you do to Rey?"

"*Tierra de diatomeas*," El Tigre said.

The gorilla mask looked puzzled. "What is diatomaceous earth?"

"It's a sedimentary rock, very soft, but very abrasive. Comes from fossils. Fossilized diatoms. Prickly stuff. Used for a lot of things, but it can tear up the soft skins of slugs and the shells of insects, so it gets used for pest control. I just rubbed Rey the wrong way with it."

Juan looked at El Tigre as though he'd just heard a lecture in ancient Greek. "Huh."

El Tigre looked around. "This place looks like hell."

El Puño grunted, surveyed the street: the demolished automobiles, the dead gangsters, the walls pocked by gunfire, the shattered windows, the broken caskets in front of the *funeraria*. "No," he said, "no it doesn't. Not at all."

He stumbled to Juan's car, climbed in the passenger side. "Come on, Cop. Don't you sell shoes? I need shoes to go with my new clothes. I want to get out of your town."

Juan looked surprised, then hurried over and drove away.

Dr. Zaius looked at El Tigre. "Now what?"

El Tigre scrubbed his face with both hands. "I need clothes, too, but Juan didn't make me an offer."

"I'll help you find a shop. Or maybe there's a tailor in town." He eyed the closed shop beside the hotel.

"And I need to get Otis home, but my car was bombed." He gestured at the dead gangsters. "Probably by those guys. I recognize a couple of them. Members of The Criminal Body. I stomped on members of The Hand a few days ago." He shook his head. "A few days ago? I need some sleep."

They approached Otis. "How are you feeling, Otis? Well enough to travel?"

"Hey, Blue Tiger. I think I'm staying here."

"What?"

Carmel raised her face to El Tigre. "I will take care of him. I will be his nurse. He is brave, a normal man facing those evil ones, not a grandstanding showoff like you and El Puño de Bronce."

Dr. Zaius started to speak, but El Tigre touched his arm.

83

Carmel turned back to Otis. "He needs tender care. I will take care of him. He will be fine."

"Thanks, El Tigre," Otis said. "I'll get back home in a few weeks. Can you watch my place?"

"Okay," El Tigre said. "I'm sorry I got you into this, Otis."

"Hey, don't worry, Tiger." Otis smiled. "Everything is cool."

El Tigre nodded. He led Dr. Zaius away.

"Let's get you some clothes," the gorilla-man said. "And I can drive you home, too."

"In that Jeep?" El Tigre stopped. He remembered the roller-coaster ride he'd had with Dr. Zaius last night. "Thank you very much. That's a generous offer. I tell you what, I'll drive home. You can ride. Then I'll make you a great dinner before you leave."

"Hey, that sounds good."

After a moment, he started walking again. "Come on. I need a bath, too, before I put on clean clothes. We didn't check out of the hotel yet."

"But the front of the hotel got shot up. You think he'll let you take a bath there?"

"I'll pay him for a bath and repairs, both." El Tigre grunted as a twinge shot through his ribs. "It'll be worth it."


CHAPTER TWENTY-FIVE

Four days later, Red Shirt sat at a table in the dark bar that stood on the way to the junkyard. A man named Oscar joined him at the table. He, also, was now too drunk to stand.

Oscar pointed at the bottle on the table. He couldn't read the bottle's label. "What are you drinking?"

Red Shirt looked at the bottle. He couldn't read the label, either. "I don't remember."

There was a flash of light as the door opened and someone entered, then the door closed. The normal dimness returned to the saloon's interior.

The figure took on features as the customers' eyes again adjusted to the lack of brightness. The newcomer was stooped, although he didn't appear to be elderly. He wore a ribbed undershirt, and the exposed flesh of his arms and torso was flaccid and seemed to hang from his bones.

He shuffled behind the bar for a broom and dustpan, then began sweeping the floor. He moved in a listless trudge around each table, dodging the drinkers at the bar.

When he reached Red Shirt's table, he bent close enough for Oscar to see his features plainly.

His face, the skin across his shoulders and arms—all were pocked, scarred as though from a disease. Even in the low light, Oscar could see the young man's color was a sick-looking yellow.

The sweeper moved away. Occasionally he had difficulties operating the broom.

Oscar asked Red Shirt, "Who is that?"

"Reynaldo Rey."

"Really?"

Red Shirt nodded.

"What happened to him?"

Red Shirt ground his teeth. He reached, drank right from the bottle.

Oscar kept talking. "I heard he moved into *la bruja*'s house. Went crazy and killed all her animals. The ones that didn't run away."

Rey finally dumped the debris from the dustpan into a bin, put away the broom. The bartender handed him a few coins and a shot glass. Rey poured the contents of the glass down his throat, then shuffled out the door.

After the darkness had settled comfortably into the room again, Oscar rested his head on the table. "Huh."

Red Shirt drank from the bottle. "That Rey. *Una bala perdida.*"


CHAPTER TWENTY-SIX

El Tigre Azul and Dr. Zaius took a week to get to El Tigre's aunt's house.

A number of adventures had distracted them from driving directly to where El Tigre was living.

Two men had stolen a tanker truck filled with gasoline. The two fighters had tracked down the truck, apprehended the thieves and handed them over to the police, and returned the truck to the owner.

Three other men had robbed a restaurant, a bank, and an ice cream delivery truck. El Tigre and Dr. Zaius detoured from their travels to hunt the gang. They located the looters' hideout, then pounded the three men when they started shooting at the two fighters. El Tigre and Dr. Zaius turned the crooks over to the police. They also recovered the money from the restaurant and bank. The ice cream had already been gobbled down by the thieves before the fighters arrived.

They rested from their various labors by sleeping all day at a motor court.

As they prepared to leave, someone invited them to sign autographs at a motion picture showing that night.

So they finally arrived at the aunt's house.

When he entered, El Tigre found a letter from his aunt on the kitchen table:

*Nephew,*

*I've gone to Sao Paulo on a birding trip. I'll be back in three weeks.*
*You didn't take the garbage out.*

*I don't understand why you can't be more dependable.*
*Love*

Auntie never signed her letters.

El Tigre sighed.

"Settle in," he directed. Then he cooked steaks, potatoes, and made a big salad. He and Dr. Zaius ate without speaking until all the plates were bare. And El Tigre watched closely, but he just couldn't figure out how Dr. Zaius ate while wearing that mask and managed not to make a mess.

"You did good out there on the road," El Tigre said.

"Thank you, El Tigre," Dr. Zaius said. "I hope I may be as great a crime fighter as you some day."

"I'm not sure *great* is the word I would use." He still had aches and pains from his battle with Rey the Octopus.

"You never told me what happened in the *funeraria*." The eyebrows rose on the gorilla mask. "I heard *la bruja* scream."

El Tigre looked at his empty plate. "The world is full of evil that's easy to reach out and grab. It's everywhere. Just like those bad men we pounded this week." He looked up at Dr. Zaius. "Then there is another evil. Evil that is otherworldly. It infects this world. It makes those men bad. There is an otherworldly goodness, too. With the help of what is holy, we can resist the evil infection. But the otherworldly evil is too big for us to fight. Our fists are too small. Even the evil ones here, they think they are its equal or greater. But when the bad guys meet the Big Evil—they can't handle it, either."

He was quiet a moment. Dr. Zaius asked, "That's why I heard *la bruja* scream?"

El Tigre nodded. "Only Holiness can battle the Big Evil. And Holiness will defeat it in the end of all things. But until then, we're around to fight the little evils." He swirled some red wine in his glass. "The little evils seem like big evils here in our world. But when our little evils face the Big Evil—or the Holiness of God—they realize how very small they are." He downed what remained in the glass.

Dr. Zaius stared at El Tigre a few moments. Then he nodded. "Okay."

They washed dishes, cleaned the kitchen, then Dr. Zaius announced, "I must go home."

"You're welcome to use the guest room."

"No, I better see to my own affairs now."

"Thank you for the transportation," El Tigre said.

"My pleasure! I had great fun chasing bad men and pounding them. I look forward to getting together to do it again!"

They were outside the house. Dr. Zaius had climbed into the driver's seat of the Jeep. He placed a pair of black sunshades over the eyeholes of his mask.

El Tigre heard a cat crying. It sat in front of Otis' home. When it saw El Tigre looking its way, it padded over to the fighter.

He lifted it, began to stoke its back. "Hungry, huh?" he said. "Otis' cat. I hope Otis is okay."

Dr. Zaius smiled. "He looked very happy when we left."

El Tigre thought of Carmel bending over Otis, holding his hand. "Yeah."

"Say, you know who that Carmel is?"

El Tigre looked at Dr. Zaius.

"I heard the doctor and the clerk talking. She's *la bruja*'s granddaughter."

El Tigre gazed again at the cat. He thought of Carmel bent over Otis like a cat over an injured mouse or a bird. "Hm."

The gorilla-man waved, roared off down the road.

El Tigre carried the cat inside. "Let's feed you, cat. I'm not sure when your daddy will be home."

The cat purred.

El Tigre was tired, but he doubted he would sleep well so long as he thought about Otis under Carmel's care.

"Ah, witches," he said. He recalled El Puño's comment: "I hate witches."

El Tigre placed a saucer of milk on the kitchen floor. He watched the cat settle in, heard the little noises as it lapped up the milk.

El Tigre reclined in the big chair before the TV. He sat staring at the blank screen, not yet willing to power on the set. He felt his fatigued muscles loosen, felt his form relax into the cushioned shape of the chair.

He closed his eyes.

"I think I hate witches, too."

*For Martha Ann*

NOTES

[1] *machine of engineered grace*—The mechanical beauty of typewriters is celebrated by a collector of these remarkable machines on a web site, *Machines of Loving Grace*. The URL is www.machinesoflovinggrace.com.

[2] This notion of someone being lost in an expansive parking lot comes from "Trek," a story by Barry Hannah that appears in *Long, Last, Happy: New and Selected Stories*, published by Grove Press, 2010.

[3] John Glanton was a mercenary who led a band of scalpers and murderers through Mexico and the Southwest United States. The gang is the focus of Cormac McCarthy's 1985 novel, *Blood Meridian*.

# { 2 }

# The Seine Witch

*La Seine Sorcière*

CHAPTER ONE

So this is where he lived!

El Tigre Azul stood on the sidewalk staring at the building across the street: 132 Boulevard Richard-Lenoir.

It was a handsome building, he thought, although smaller than he'd anticipated. Four stories rose above the ground floor, which housed shops. It was an odd-shaped building, which El Tigre realized once he'd circled it and gazed from the sidewalks opposite the structure: The only building on a triangular postage-stamp island amid the busy Paris streets, it had nearly a triangular footprint, but the two acute angles had been flattened so the shape was actually a five-sided polygon. A distinctive home for its famous resident.

Since the block on which the building stood was small, perhaps the apartments within the structure were small as well? That might be right, El Tigre considered. A cozy, homey place for the bearish detective.

The Paris home of Commissaire Maigret.

It was handsome and sturdy, as he'd imagined. El Tigre's companion, Louis, rattled off details:

"The architects call this Second Empire style, which grew popular during the reign of Emperor Napoleon III in the Nineteenth Century. A liberal use of decorative elements, such as ornate corbels and balcony balustrades, as you can see. The mansard roof and the dormer windows—"

As Louis chattered away, El Tigre stood on the corner and grinned while he stared at the structure. Buses whooshed and wheezed as they rushed past. Cars beeped and cyclists ting-tingled their bells. No one seemed to notice that a broad-shouldered man in a light gray suit stood on the street wearing a blue-and-black mask that covered nearly his entire head.

El Tigre paid no mind to the whirling traffic and the reek of exhaust. He was simply near-dizzy with happiness to be seeing the great detective's home.

He wondered how he'd be received if he knocked at the apartment's door? Would it be rented only to residents who were deaf, so they'd not notice the entreaties of Simenon's zealous readers? Or would they be crazed by the constant interruptions to their days, and would they meet unasked-for visitors with a grimace and a raised truncheon?

A small park filled with trees and flowering shrubs lay at El Tigre's back. A nice enough view for Maigret when he might peer out a window.

Live-recorded music—some rock-and-roll thing, with lively guitar playing—blared out from an open window. Not the sort of thing El Tigre preferred. He was sure it wasn't in Inspector Maigret's stack of albums. The wrestler turned to his companion and asked about it.

Louis D'Arnot served as the luchador's guide and interpreter. He was shorter than El Tigre and slenderly built, but the beginning of a little belly pushed against his yellow turtleneck shirt, although he was still a young man, not yet thirty years old. His hair was black and cut conservatively except for long sideburns that reached his jawline. For a young person who wore a blue-and-red plaid jacket over a yellow shirt and green slacks, he presented a very serious demeanor. He'd been assigned to El Tigre by the luchador's Parisian host, and the pair had gotten along quite well since their introduction a day ago.

As Louis listened and thought, his lower lip rose and covered his upper lip and nearly reached the base of his nose. The right eyebrow burrowed down and shadowed his eye, while the other rose and lifted his hairline. His expression worried El Tigre, who asked, "Have you taken a bite of something foul?" He spoke slowly and enunciated sharply. "Can't you swallow it?"

Louis continued to make faces.

"You can spit it out. I won't be offended." El Tigre looked around the street. "Although I'm not so sure about your countrymen."

Louis' face recovered its normal expression. He didn't spit, and El Tigre hadn't noticed that he'd swallowed. In fact, he smiled at the wrestler. "Cream," he said.

"Que es eso?"

"The guitarist is Eric Clapton," Louis explained. "The song is 'Crossroads.' The performance is by a band named Cream."

"Ah." El Tigre stared at the building and listened to the song. "I prefer Frank Sinatra. And Dean Martin."

"Oh. *Oui.*"

El Tigre closed his eyes to open his mind's eye and to focus and shut out the noise of the street and the smells of exhaust and garbage. Closed off in this way, he recalled his retreats from the cities and the clammer of men and women and children when he would escape to the timbered mountains of Durango. He would sit in the shade of a tree and listen to the wind feather through the green needles and, when he had waited long enough and nearly exhausted his patience, he would hear the wind tumble grit over the surface of the ground. He would fish in streams and at night stare at the currents of the stars until vertigo made him place his palms on the ground to steady his relationship with gravity. In the afternoons he would laze under a tree and read chapters of a cheap Maigret paperback book.

He opened his eyes when he felt a hand. Louis gripped his elbow and looked at him with concern. "Are you dizzy?" he asked. "You were leaning toward the automobiles. They're moving."

El Tigre smiled. "*Gracias*. I'm fine. Which way to headquarters?"

Louis recovered his smile. He gestured along the sidewalk. "Follow me."

El Tigre took a last glance at Maigret's sturdy-looking home and commenced to follow Louis.

Like any city, Paris was loud and crowded and colorful. What stood out to El Tigre was the ubiquitous appearance of youthful fashion—so much more than he was accustomed to seeing in Mexico City. Bright colors, paisley, swirling lines, very short skirts, sunglasses with big lenses. Passing life on the everyday street was like a carnival procession. He felt a bit self-conscious, thinking his conservative gray suit made him conspicuous on the street. He gave no thought about his mask perhaps being unusual.

A flutter of surprised delight at his presence in Paris—a place he'd never supposed he would visit—kept El Tigre's steps light and lively. He had been invited to Paris by a film director, Pierre Savant. They had met in Mexico City, where the director was participating in a cultural exchange event.

Their encounter had been an accident.

El Tigre had been a step away from entering a bakery to buy a bag of *conchas* when he collided with a man who dashed out of the shop. Both fell to the sidewalk. When the running man saw who he'd struck, he shouted a foul word and jumped to his feet. He was limping and carrying a burlap bag whose sides were stretched out by whatever was inside.

As El Tigre had gotten up, the stranger leapt onto a motor scooter. He started it and zoomed into traffic.

By this time workers were wailing inside the bakery. "*Robo! Nos han robado!*"

El Tigre started running after the robber.

"Hey! Stop!"

People on the sidewalks saw the big masked battler hurrying and shouting and stepped out of his way. Children cheered as he flew past.

"Get him El Tigre! Get him! *Vamos!*"

Despite his exertions, the scooter was getting farther away. A bicyclist whipped past El Tigre, stopped and offered him his ride. The wrestler paused long enough to mount the bike and started peddling. "*Gracias, amigo.*" He wobbled and tottered a few yards—the bike's seat was locked into place a little lower than was suitable for El Tigre— and then he established a rhythm and took off.

After several minutes, the thief spotted his pursuer in his rearview mirror. He squawked a syllable of fright, and then he tried to coax more speed out of the scooter's engine, but the throttle was wide open.

He squawked again.

He turned to the right and wove the scooter between cars, desperate to lose the resolute fiend of justice behind him.

El Tigre shouted and rang the bike's shrill little bell, trying to be heard above the car horns and tire squeals and revving engines. Despite his quarry's efforts, El Tigre got closer with each minute of the pursuit.

A woman started to cross the street but then spotted the rushing scooter approaching. Startled, she dropped her canvas tote and stepped back.

The scooter buzzed past with a rush of wind.

The tote's braided rope handles stood up from the bag's top. As he clickety-whirred past, El Tigre reached and snatched up the tote from the pavement.

Its owner shook her fist at his diminishing form and yelled, "Thief!"

El Tigre peddled madly and swung the tote in a circle over his head. The chase was approaching Chapultepec Park, where competing traffic was less hazardous. With the scooter clearly in sight ahead of him, he released the tote and flung it forward like an improvised bolo-sling. The bag wheeled through the air and smacked into the back of the robber's neck. Surprised more than hurt, he released the handlebar grips and windmilled his arms. The scooter spun and dropped and skidded, and its rider tumbled and rolled and slid across the cracked pavement. He came to a stop at the foot of a wide staircase that led up to doors for the Museo de Arte Moderno. On the final step of this staircase, only a few inches from the dazed and gasping thief, were the feet of two people at the head of a larger group that had just exited the museum after a film showing, a question-and-answer session, and an hour of cocktails. One pair of these feet belonged to Pierre Savant, who looked down in surprise at the human bundle murmuring in his path.

El Tigre rolled up and braked the bike and rang its bell. He dismounted and kneeled by the robber and checked his pulse and raised his eyelids to see his eyes. He looked at the man and woman on the steps and the crowd behind them and said, "He is fine, just a bit knocked around. Please call an ambulance and the police. He has robbed a bakery." El Tigre tugged the burlap bag from the man's grip, for the thief hadn't released it during the entire chase. He looked inside and saw a nest of money.

A shout from the man on the nearby step made El Tigre shift his attention: "*Je vous connais!*"

The woman at the man's side translated, "He says he knows you. He is Pierre Savant."

El Tigre looked at the man's face, then he answered, "I don't know him. Who is he?"

"A film director. From France," the woman answered. Even in heels she came only to Savant's shoulder. She had long black hair and flashing dark eyes and wore a navy dress with tasteful lines suitable for a professional cocktail hour.

Savant had continued talking with excitement and gestures. He wore a black beret that couldn't contain the thick wavy hair that covered his ears, a black turtleneck shirt, dark green tropical-weight jacket, black trousers, and white rubber-soled tennis shoes. The woman said, "He's seen your movies."

El Tigre stood and smiled. "That's someone else." While the woman explained that in French, the director took the battler's hand and shook it with vigor and clear delight. He showed all his teeth as he spoke on and on without pausing to breathe.

The woman listened a moment and blinked before saying, "Señor Savant doesn't care that the movies are about someone else. He's heard about your war with *Le Corps Criminal*, eh, *El Cuerpo Criminal*."

"Ah, yes." He looked at the woman while Savant kept pumping his hand and talking. "What's your name?"

"Lola Soriano." Without a pause, she continued her work with Savant. "Señor Savant wants you to join us for dinner."

El Tigre looked at the people behind the director and his interpreter. Numbering about thirty men and women, they all stared and listened carefully as though they were attending the performance of a stage play and wanted not to miss a single word of dialog. "I must wait for the police—"

Lola interrupted: "He says that's fine, and he'd like to see your interactions with the authorities. He also has questions for you. Do you always work on a bicycle? Is a bag of cabbage heads your usual weapon of choice? Do you have more than one bicycle you use for chasing criminals? You don't have to answer now, but we can discuss these and other things during our meal."

During this dinner, which El Tigre joined—as much to continue talking with Lola as to answer Pierre Savant's questions—the director insisted the wrestler come to Paris. "Señor Savant says he will pay your way and you will be his guest."

"I cannot speak French," El Tigre said. "And I see Señor Savant does not speak Spanish. We'll need a translator."

Lola smiled. "So you will."

So El Tigre left the director's party that night both charmed and looking forward to his trip. He didn't see Savant or Lola again before the director returned to France.

Two weeks later, when El Tigre landed at the new Aéroport de Paris-Charles-de-Gaulle in the suburbs of Paris at Roissy-en-France, he looked all around for Lola. Instead, he was met by Louis.

El Tigre left the past behind when Louis stopped at the Pont Saint-Michel and waved across the street to a massive building that wrapped around the corner of the Quai des Orfèvres and the Boulevard du Palais and overlooked the Seine River, which lay behind the two men.

Home of the Police Judiciaire de Paris.

Commissaire Maigret's workplace.

Louis was busy explaining how the architectural style of the structure before the two men matched that of Maigret's apartment building.

But, El Tigre thought, on a monumental scale quite different from the other site.

El Tigre interrupted the architecture lesson: "Can we go inside?"

Louis started to make that something-foul-in-the-mouth face when he stopped and smiled instead. "It is a public building. *Oui*."

"Let's go."

Louis led them across the street and to a door. El Tigre was nearly across the threshold when he collided with a group of men on their way out. In the lead was a man with thick black hair and a mustache obscuring his upper lip. He wore a plaid yellow jacket over green slacks. And a very angry look.

When he ran into El Tigre he bounced back with an exclamation whose tone matched his expression. He looked up at the staggering wrestler and surprise replaced the anger on his face. For only a moment. Then he shouted something else. El Tigre didn't need Louis' help to know it meant nothing pleasant.

El Tigre held the door while the party hurried out and left in a small fleet of unmarked cars.

Inside the precinct, El Tigre looked around. "I'd always heard how friendly Parisians are. Guess they really are." He asked Louis, "What's going on here? Lots of excitement. Well, even for a police station."

"Oh, this is exciting," Louis said. "Many people have been disappearing. Near the Seine."

"So?"

"A report says they floated to the surface of the river. Twelve of them."

CHAPTER TWO

El Tigre Azul wasn't entirely sure why Pierre Savant had wanted him to come to Paris. This was his first full day in the city, and Louis had said Monsieur Savant wanted his guest to join him for dinner, but he didn't know when that would be. So Louis was acting as the visiting wrestler's tour guide in the City of Lights.

Finding out the site that had the police so excited wasn't hard to do: El Tigre and Louis hailed a taxi cab. After they climbed in, Louis asked the driver where all the cops were going. The driver's radio had directed all the city's cabs to stay away from Pont Alexandre III. "They must be going there," the man said.

Once Louis explained this to El Tigre, the wrestler said, "That's where we're going."

Something overtook Louis' face that wasn't the something-foul-in-the-mouth look. El Tigre thought the man had been struck by an acute attack of gastric distress. The wrestler asked, "Are you okay? Do you need a hospital?"

He quickly understood this sign of pain was Louis' way of looking dumbfounded.

"We cannot go there, Monsieur Le Tigre," Louis pleaded. "La Police are there. It is a, uh, *scène de crime.*"

The driver's head was twisted around and his eyes were wide while he witnessed this conversation in the back of his cab. El Tigre glanced at him before asking Louis, "It's at a bridge?"

"*Oui. Si.*"

"It is a public place?"

"*Si. Oui.*"

"Let's go."


CHAPTER THREE

Pont Alexandre III was perhaps the most magnificent bridge that crossed the Seine. It probably was the most magnificent bridge in Paris.

Louis didn't quite pant during the ride to the crime scene, but acting as tour guide and reciting facts seemed to relieve some of his anxiety about intruding on the members of the police force while they were about their business.

"Thirty-seven bridges and footbridges span the Seine, connecting the Left Bank to the Right Bank," he said. "The oldest is Pont Neuf. It was built by order of Henri IV in 1578."

El Tigre nodded. "*Si*, that's old."

"Pont Alexandre III was built between 1896 and 1900 in the Beaux-Arts style."

"Not Second Empire?"

"*Non*."

"No mansard roof?"

"Monsieur Le Tigre, it is a bridge." Louis' eyes were half-lidded and his shoulders slumped as he said these words. El Tigre wasn't sure if this was the interpreter's expression of exasperation or simply of sadness about his companion's stupidity.

"*Cierto*, it is a bridge," El Tigre conceded. "I am eager to see it."

Louis looked sadder. "*Oui*."

The cab dropped off the pair a block away from the bridge. A police cordon prevented the public from approaching the bridge itself. El Tigre led the way as they descended to the Port des Champs-Élysées overlooking the river. The area was crowded with sightseers craning to watch official boats retrieving the bodies from the water. The corpses floated in a cluster below the highest point of the bridge's supporting arch. Even from this distance, El Tigre could see how bloated and pale the dead people were.

He turned to Louis, who was mesmerized by the activity on the water. "How long have these people been missing?"

"People go missing in Paris all the time," Louis said. He didn't move his gaze from the river. "But the newspapers have said there are a surprising number of missing persons reports recently. And if these people are those people, they didn't disappear as a group. Just one by one. And the newspapers say the recent epidemic began six weeks ago."

"Twelve people in six weeks?"

"Oh, more than twelve," Louis corrected him. "At least twice that many."

El Tigre felt a chill. He said a silent prayer.

"*Il a raison*," said a woman near El Tigre's left. He judged she was around forty years old. She had blond hair that streamed in the breeze and green eyes that watched him in a clear, intelligent way. She wore a white blouse with the collar turned up and a green-and-white striped skirt. She held a pad of lined paper and an ink pen. "*Tu dois être le guerrier Pierre Savant importé du Mexique.*"

El Tigre looked at Louis, who translated, "You must be the warrior Pierre Savant imported from Mexico."

The warrior bowed. "I am." He smiled and asked, "And you are?" With Louis' help, he attempted to converse with the woman. The interpreter appeared a little peeved to split his attention between watching the police boats' activities and translating for his companion's benefit, but he didn't turn away from the scenes on the river.

"Marie Dupont," she answered and extended a hand. They shook. "*L'Équipe.*"

El Tigre thought a moment. "Isn't that a sports paper?"

"*Oui.*"

"Why are you here?"

Marie smiled. "You are a sports figure, *non*?"

"I am, but why are you covering this event?"

Her smile evaporated. "One of the missing women is the fiancé of a local competitor, a popular cyclist. She may be one of those unfortunates."

El Tigre turned his gaze to the Pont Alexandre III. He scanned the faces he could see over the bridge's balustrade between the ornate Art Nouveau lamps that marched along its length. He spotted a familiar face. He asked Marie, "Who is that fellow in the plaid yellow jacket, directing activities on the bridge?"

The woman peered a few moments before responding. "Inspector Hugo Hatin. He's in charge of the investigation for the people who've gone missing the past six weeks."

"Clues?"

"Very few," Marie admitted. "One man claimed he saw a woman approach a man on Pont Neuf. She grabbed him and jumped into the river. Carried the man with her, and they didn't come back to the surface."

"What came of that?"

The reporter shook her head. "The witness was several yards away from where it happened. And it was two in the morning. And he was so drunk, he didn't tell the police his story until after he was found asleep the next morning on the Quai de Conti."

El Tigre nodded.

Marie poked his thick shoulder with the blunt end of her pen. "How about you let me interview you?"

"Me?"

"I've never interviewed a warrior from Mexico before."

"What about this?" He gestured at the boats on the Seine at their grisly work.

"That will go on all afternoon," Marie said. "The police will reveal nothing today. They will have a press conference in the morning."

"Okay." They set a time for later in the afternoon.

El Tigre nudged Louis. "Let's go back to headquarters. I want to see where the commissaire works."


CHAPTER FOUR

At 36 Quai des Orfèvres, the pair reached the limits of public access and were rebuffed. They turned around and tried a different hallway. Then a stairway. Each time, they were told to leave the area unless they had official business to conduct. Each time, they were told in a sterner tone of voice. The fifth time, they were escorted out of the building.

Dismayed but undiscouraged, Louis led him to a nearby bridge, Pont Neuf. "It does not shine in the way Pont Alexandre III does, but it has its own beauty. It is the oldest stone bridge in Paris."

"So you've said."

"Yet its name," Louis said, and El Tigre was sure if it was possible to see a twinkle in a man's eyes, he saw one in Louis' eyes, "means New Bridge."

"How clever the French are."

Following Quai des Orfèvres, they quickly reached the western point of the Île de la Cité and Pont Neuf. Louis led El Tigre across the bridge's shorter span, supported by five arches, to the Left Bank. They returned to the Île de la Cité and crossed the longer span, with seven arches, to the Right Bank before retracing their steps to the island. All the while Louis chattered about the Pont Neuf's history: its design was based on Roman architecture, and was the first bridge in Paris built without houses along its span—by order of Henri IV, who said people should be able to see the Seine from the bridge; further, it was the first bridge to include pavements for pedestrians, based on Roman roads, so those on foot would be protected from the muck churned up by wagon traffic.

Next Louis directed El Tigre down to the quai so they could cross under the arch connecting the longer span to the island. As they approached the arch, Louis stopped and pointed out the sturdy stonework and noted the decorative molding and its corbels spaced along the entire span. Attached to each corbel was a head, and each head had a particularly ugly face. "These are *mascarons*," Louis said.

"*Mascarons*?"

"*Oui.* Eh, masks. More than three hundred line both sides of Pont Neuf."

"Kinda ugly."

"*Oui. Si.* The heads of mythological creatures who lived in the fields and forests that once surrounded this island."

There were dozens of other people nearby, and all had stopped to point and peer at the *mascarons*. El Tigre noticed several of these people talking and gesturing animatedly while pointing. He looked up and asked Louis, "Do you hear something?" He strained to listen. "It's hard to hear over the traffic sounds, but there's a—a vibration, or a humming."

Puzzlement crossed Louis' face. He cupped his hands around his ears. "*Oui. Oui*! I hear it now."

El Tigre pointed. "Look!"

Tiny fissures were appearing around the mouths of the *mascarons*. The mouths of many were carved so that they were open, and the tongues of some *mascarons* protruded. The mouths of others were obscured by mustaches or beards. But as El Tigre watched, all the mouths opened wide as the humming grew louder, finally overwhelming the growls and roars of cars and trucks.

Louis trembled and ducked his head. "I hear it! I hear it! It—it hurts!"

The heads on the bridge began to shake. The pedestrians covered their ears, and most began to back away from the bridge and run out from under the arch as the sound became painful.

Then all the heads burst!

El Tigre covered Louis to protect him from the shards of stone blowing outward toward the people on the quai. Stone chips and chunks and dust rained down and pattered along the pavement. The remains of the *mascarons* tumbled and splashed into the Seine. Dust clouds floated up from the brackets where the heads had been attached. The little clouds thinned into white threads and dissipated in the breeze.

The humming was gone, replaced by the yells and screams of the injured.


CHAPTER FIVE

El Tigre and Louis entered police headquarters again. Almost immediately they encountered Inspector Hugo Hatin, who was striding quickly from deeper within the building toward the same door. By the policeman's expression, El Tigre was sure Hatin's anger was intact.

Louis bounded forward. "Ah! Inspector! We are looking for you! We have—"

Hatin ignored the little interpreter as soon as he spotted the big wrestler. "You! Again! Who parades around police headquarters in a mask? Only a freak! Get out of here, freak! Out of my sight!"

El Tigre touched Louis on the shoulder, and the two men exited the building.

"Ah, well, Monsieur Le Tigre, we tried. At least we gave our statement to the policemen at Pont Neuf."

"Yes," El Tigre agreed, "but the heads exploded on the bridge so soon after the bodies appeared farther downstream. It seems the two events might be connected in some way. I thought the inspector would want to know."

Louis sighed. "The inspector has many things on his mind already."

"That's true. It's almost time for meeting Señora Dupont."

"Señorita—eh, Mademoiselle Dupont," Louis corrected him.

"Oh. Well, it'll be okay to show up early."

A short jaunt along Rue de Harlay, which ran behind Inspector Hatin's fiefdom and the Palais de Justice, to a shop whose sign read CAFÉ RESTAURANT AUX TROIS MARCHES. It sat on the corner where Rue de Harlay met Quai de l'Horloge and faced the west façade of the Police Judiciare. El Tigre and Louis ascended the three steps that gave the café its name and found a table.

When Marie Dupont joined the pair, she asked why El Tigre had selected this place for the interview. Louis answered for him: "Monsieur Le Tigre is a great fan of the famous Commissaire Maigret. Apparently the inspector often visited this place."

Marie cocked her head and smiled. "The inspector was a frequent customer here, but not here."

"No, not Trois Marches," El Tigre said. "But he called it the Brasserie Dauphine. But the name doesn't matter so much as the place."

Marie nodded to the wrestler's arm. "Your coat sleeve is torn. Have you been fighting our local champions?"

"No," Louis said, "we were attacked by heads!"

Marie, puzzled, turned from one man to the other. She waited for an explanation.

El Tigre started: "I was hit by a head."

"What?"

"The *mascarons* exploded."

"You were there?"

Louis was nearly panting as he recalled the scene. "Yes, and it was terrible. Terrible!"

Together, Marie's companions described what they'd witnessed and experienced. They included their disappointing encounter with Inspector Hatin.

Marie waved away their complaint as of no importance. "Policemen have no imagination." She waved for a server to take their orders.

"Reporters have imaginations?" El Tigre asked. "I thought you dealt in facts only."

The woman laughed. "If the level of competition in a sporting event is particularly dull, it is the job of the writer to make a ho-hum match exciting to read about."

The three placed their orders, and Marie then said, "That's not true about cops having no imagination. I'm sure some of them do. But not Inspector Hatin. No imagination."

"How do you know?"

"I interview a different luminary now and then about their sporting interests," Marie said. "Hugo Hatin was my subject a few months ago. The man's mind is drab as chalk. But he does have an interest that is on the verge of passion for the Tour de France." She changed topics: "Have you heard any explanation for the *mascarons* exploding? Is it anarchists? War protesters?"

Louis shook his head.

El Tigre said, "No one has an explanation. And it was every head on the bridge."

Shock touched Marie's face. "That's—let's see—that's three hundred eighty-one sculpted heads on Pont Neuf. All of them?"

Louis nodded.

El Tigre gestured vaguely. "I felt the *mascarons* were—I don't know, trying to tell us something."

Marie's words carried a skeptical tone. "You think the *mascarons* were talking to you because you wear a mask?"

"No, I don't know about that." He paused before continuing. "I think it has something to do with the bodies that floated to the surface of the river."

Marie straightened in her chair, attentive. "Go on."

"I don't really know." El Tigre struggled to use words for Louis to say that wouldn't sound foolish to this smart woman. "I've seen many strange things in Mexico. This felt like one of those strange things."

The writer turned to Louis. "What about you? What do you think?"

"It was definitely strange. Strange and terrible. Terrible!"

"Calm down!" Marie commanded. "Have a drink." She looked at El Tigre. "Now you. What else?"

"That's all." He sighed. "It's too bad. If they were truly going to tell us something, it's too late. They're just powder and grit now."

"Pish!" Marie waved away El Tigre's comments. "The bridge was rebuilt in the 1850s. All the original *mascarons* were replaced then. The ones you saw blowing up were reproductions."

El Tigre glanced at Louis and then said, "So?"

"So the original heads still exist. If the copies couldn't talk to you, maybe the originals can. They're housed at the Musée Carnavalet and the Château d'Écouen. Every Parisian knows that."

After hearing Louis translate this last sentence, El Tigre looked at him. The interpreter appeared not to notice his gaze, as if he'd not heard the very words that had come from his mouth. Instead, he sat up straight and announced, "Ah, here's our order!"

After paying, Marie marched the two men to the street and hailed a cab. "We'll go to the Musée Carnavalet. It's closer."

They crossed the Seine on the Boulevard du Palais to the Right Bank and soon were deposited before a sprawling renaissance mansion in the Marais district at 23 Rue de Sévigné. Marie led the two men inside, where she snatched up a map from a kiosk, unfolded it, ran her gaze over it, then snapped her fingers. "*Venez*! Come along."

And they marched into the depths of the museum.

El Tigre was dazzled by his surroundings—sculptures, paintings, jewelry, photographs, drawings, textiles, artifacts dug up from the pre-Roman mud—but Marie allowed him no time to dawdle.

They entered a smaller room dedicated to the Pont Neuf. Sepia photographs and stereograph cards, paintings and drawings with the bridge and its details were hung on three walls. On the fourth, ten stone heads were mounted in a horizontal line. They stared at whomever gazed at them.

*Mascarons*. Original *mascarons* from the Pont Neuf.

Louis read a card attached to the wall: "The Pont Neuf *mascarons* are attributed to Renaissance sculptor Germain Pilon, born circa 1525 to 1535 and died 1590. The *mascarons* represent mythical creatures with fierce or humorous expressions intended to frighten away evil spirits." He turned and looked at the leering wall. "I'm not sure about evil spirits, but they frighten me."

Close like this, El Tigre could see just how disturbing the faces truly were. He wondered how the artist had managed to come up with such a variety of ugly features. And imagine: three hundred eighty-one of them! Each one different!

He noticed that Louis had sidled up to him, and positioned himself a step behind, putting the fighter between the interpreter and the wall of faces.

Other visitors were meandering through the museum, but none had ventured into this room. El Tigre knew people were somewhere outside the door, but he couldn't hear them. The silence here was so complete, he could hear the slight sounds of breathing from both of his companions.

Marie broke the quiet: *"Bien? N'importe quoi?"*

El Tigre could barely make out Louis' whisper: "Well? Anything?"

"No," the fighter said, "I don't feel—"

A gritting sound cracked the quiet. Like rough stones slowly grinding together.

The hair rose on El Tigre's arms. He could feel Louis standing very close behind him. He glanced at Marie, who had also shifted nearer to the fighter, and who stood stiffly at attention as she stared at the wall of heads.

The air changed, grew very cool. The light in the room dimmed. The quality of sounds also changed, as if the trio stood within a cavern and a hollow effect had joined the gritting noise. Plumes of breath rose from El Tigre's mask and curled away. Then he noticed a new scent in the air: He smelled water. He recognized the smell of the Seine River.

Then the stone heads spoke.

All of them.

In unison.

Their eyes bugged and their tongues lashed the air. They showed their strange teeth.

And they spoke:

*We are the witnesses.*

*Listen closely.*

*A creature is performing evil in our city.*

*A witch is dishonoring our bridge.*

*Alison Legrand came from Ardennes with nine others.*

*Witches condemned to die.*

*They were summoned to le Parlement de Paris for appeals.*

*She saw our new bridge and said it was beautiful.*

*Nine were released with punishments.*

*Alison Legrand was executed.*

*She cursed the city on the gallows.*

*She died.*

*Her spirit came to our bridge.*

*It lived there.*

*We fought her presence but she would not leave.*

*She hates Pont Alexandre III.*

*Her jealousy has given her form again.*

*Her rage destroys those who admire Pont Alexandre III.*

*We are the witnesses.*

Then there was silence, deep and suffocating. Slowly the room's original environment returned: the smell of air-conditioning replaced that of the river, the cavernous reverberation faded, the light resumed its normal level.

El Tigre noticed his limbs trembling. He turned and saw Louis stretched out on the floor—the man had fainted. He kneeled to tend to the interpreter and glanced at the reporter.

Marie remained stock still. She was pale, and the fighter could tell she clenched her jaw fiercely.

"What did you hear?" El Tigre asked. "Spanish?"

Marie shook herself and released the tension in her limbs before responding. "No. No, French."

"Hm."

She whipped to look at him. "I understood you. I—"

"Yes, and I just understood you. Are you speaking Spanish?"

"No, not at all." Marie looked terribly flustered.

"And I'm not speaking French."

Louis was soon roused. As El Tigre helped him to his feet, Marie asked, "How did that happen?"

"I don't know." El Tigre held one of Louis' arms and Marie the other as they made their way to the museum's exit. "I have a friend. He has seen—he has experienced stranger things than I have. These encounters have given him—I'm not sure what to call it. An aura? An affinity for strangeness? I have been with him when some of these unexplainable events have occurred. Perhaps some of his strange radiation now clings to me. And that invisible glow encourages this sort of interaction with the inexplicable."

Outside, Louis breathed deeply as he worked to replace what he imagined was the tainted museum air in his system with normal, ordinary Parisian air.

Marie gazed at El Tigre with a thoughtful expression. "*Qu'est-ce qu'on fait maintenant?*"

He looked at her. "Eh, *qué dijiste?*"

The mysterious untangling of their native tongues in their ears was gone.

He patted Louis' shoulder. "Louis, are you up to translating again?"

"*Oui!*" Louis drew himself up. He put on the appearance of a man who was in the fittest form of health. "I would never shirk my work."

"Good, good," El Tigre said. "Tell Marie I think we should go to the bridge. I need to find this witch and stop her."

Louis deflated a bit. "Are you sure?"

"*Si.*"

Louis explained to Marie. "Are you sure?"

El Tigre nodded. "This terror must stop. This witch will continue murdering people if she's not stopped."

Marie was skeptical. "How do you know—what we heard is true? They're just a bunch of stone heads!"

"And they talked." The fighter grinned at her.

"So what will you do?"

El Tigre shrugged. "I have no idea. But something will come to me when I'm there."

Marie scowled at him. The breeze blew her hair into her face, and she muttered a grunt of aggravation and pushed the strands behind her ears. "You believe that?"

"I always do."

The reporter clenched her fists. "This is insane. This is irrational. How can this happen in Twentieth Century Paris?"

"I've found the world doesn't know it's supposed to follow rational rules as athletes do in their sports," El Tigre said.

Marie puffed a little explosion of derision. "Your bad analogy doesn't convince me this is the proper thing to do." She twisted the sole of one shod foot on the pavement in frustration. She'd never encountered such a situation, and her anxiety about its irreality made her extremely uncomfortable. "*Zut*," she finally said, "I'm coming too." She looked at Louis. "That means you have to come along as well."

It was El Tigre's turn to frown. "Are you sure about that?"

"Yes!" Marie nearly shouted.

The fighter turned to Louis. "You don't have to go, Louis."

Louis brought up his chin. "I am not a brave man in the way you are, Monsieur Le Tigre. But I told you, I never shirk my work."

El Tigre gave the interpreter a warm smile. "Very well, *amigo*. Let's go find this Alison Legrand."

Marie hailed a taxi. "The nearest thing to a river witch I've heard about is Sequana."

The men looked at the reporter and waited for an explanation.

"All Parisians know about Sequana," she said.

Louis shook his head and shrugged.

Marie sighed. "Sequana is the goddess of the Seine. She was honored by the Celts who settled in Gaul long before the Romans came."

"What does she do?" El Tigre asked.

A puzzled expression crossed Marie's face. "What do any of those old gods do? They sit here and there like statues and birds perch on them." She shook her head. "There's a famous bronze of Sequana. It's only so tall—maybe thirty, thirty-two centimeters—and she's standing in a duck-shaped boat."

"A duck-shaped boat?"

"Yes."

"What does she look like?"

Marie was puzzled. "A beautiful woman. Quite regal looking." She looked at El Tigre.

El Tigre nodded. "I think the gods of the Inca and Maya are depicted more realistically. They are beyond human comprehension. They look like monsters."

Marie shrugged. "She's a goddess. The spirit of the Seine. Other than that, I don't think she does anything."

As a cab braked before them, El Tigre said, "She's letting a dead witch get away with murder."


CHAPTER SIX

After the group climbed into the Citroen taxi, Marie changed their immediate plan.

She remembered another interview subject—a priest, Father Jean-Louis Voillaume—who was a football enthusiast and infamous locally for performing an exorcism a few years ago. She directed the driver to Voillaume's residence.

Once there, after they helped the priest resolve his consternation at the sight of a large, masked man in a torn gray suit appearing at his door, the trio explained their reason for requesting his assistance.

Father Voillaume was in his fifties, a tall, gaunt man in a black suit. The top of his head was bald, and a pair of reading glasses hung on a ribbon from his neck. Many people of the free world were cutting loose from the cultural anchors that maintained the traditional social expectations for behavior, but within the priest's book-lined study, Voillaume carried the gravitas of a man who had shared the weight of his flock's burdens and expected to continue doing so. When he heard his visitors' story, the flesh around his gray eyes crinkled up and his mouth dropped open.

"Children," he said, "what you're proposing is—is horrible. This is a terrible story."

While Louis translated for El Tigre, Marie asked, "You'll come with us?"

The priest looked at her, and then the two men, sternly. "You must not do this thing."

Louis stared at Voillaume. El Tigre nudged the interpreter. "What did he say? What did he say?"

Marie, unfazed, asked, "Why?"

Voillaume cleared his throat, sat back in his upholstered chair and knitted his fingers together. "If these—strange things you've told me are true, then you are facing something devilish and evil. Satanic. And I look at you—a timid man who repeats words to a man in a mask and a woman who talks to people and writes their words for others to read—and I see people who are not prepared for dealing with what you describe."

When El Tigre head Louis' words, the fighter turned to Voillaume. "Father, do you believe in God?"

Hearing Louis' translation, the priest looked shocked. He stood up and straightened his shoulders. "I am a man of God. I am a called servant of the most high Lord of all creation."

El Tigre smiled. "I am a believer as well. And so you understand the Power on which I rely."

"You are a man in a mask," Voillaume protested. "An entertainer."

"I have seen—and battled—many strange things," El Tigre said. He remained calm. "Every person in this parish battles evils each day. Whether they are small or large evils doesn't matter. Evil is evil."

Marie allowed only a slight pause before she said, "Go with us. You've done this before."

"No," Father Voillaume shook his head, "nothing like this. The rite of exorcism is nothing like you see in a movie. And it is nothing that anyone undertakes lightly and unprepared between trips to the concession stand."

Marie stood. "Then go with us."

The priest waved aside the request. "I cannot condone your actions. I cannot participate. Please go. Know that I will pray for your safety and protection." As Father Voillaume ushered them from the study, he gave his parting word: "Go with God."

At the street, El Tigre waved for a cab. Marie and Louis' disappointment was palpable.

"So the priest won't go with us," the fighter said. "But now we've got something better."

Louis looked up at him. "What?"

"God."

CHAPTER SEVEN

During the ride to Pont Alexandre III, the driver said, "Radio says preliminary reports from the police identify the twelve floaters they found today as some of the missing twenty-four."

When he heard this, Louis shivered beside El Tigre. The fighter understood: The driver's report meant the museum's *mascarons* were correct. As crazy as it sounded, a dead witch wanted to discredit a bridge for—well, for some reason.

Dusk was chasing the daylight as they approached the bridge. It had been reopened to traffic, but a number of uniformed policemen patrolled its length on foot. Several civilian gawkers were also present—pointing, pausing, taking photographs, laughing at what had been the scene of a horrifying discovery only a few hours earlier. "Look at them," Louis said. Both fear and disdain poisoned his voice.

"Life is for the living," El Tigre said.

Marie scrutinized him as they walked. "You don't look like the philosophical type."

El Tigre laughed when he heard Louis' translation. "We still haven't had that interview. Who knows what you may learn?"

In the falling light, as the lamps began to glow, the fighter had to admit Pont Alexandre III certainly was a magnificent sight. With its many arches and Romanesque stonework, Pont Neuf served as a weighty anchor to the past. However, the Beaux-Arts ornamentation of Pont Alexandre III, its gleaming gilt-bronze statues of winged figures atop the tall socles at the ends of the bridge, and the massive nude copper nymphs centered at the top of the long arch, all brought to reality a fairy tale fantasy that otherwise lived only in the mind. Twisted as it might have been, El Tigre could almost understand how a self-styled champion for the simpler Pont Neuf might be jealous of Pont Alexandre III's glittering showiness.

El Tigre stopped by the nymphs to look down at the river. Marie and Louis joined him, one on each side. The lamplight and the glow from the city flickered and flowed over the water's moving surface like a living, multifarious will of the wisp. Its beauty carried no hint of the horror it had disgorged that day. The wavering frets and puddles of light danced and changed places. They were mesmerizing. The sounds of passing vehicles and the voices of pedestrians receded from El Tigre's conscious.

"You!"

This voice snapped him back to his place on the bridge. El Tigre turned to see Inspector Hugo Hatin pushing past pedestrians enjoying the night views. He heard Louis squeak at the same time Marie whispered an unladylike word.

El Tigre rummaged up some passable French: "*Bonsoir, Inspecteur.*"

"*Soyez silencieux!*" Hatin jabbed a finger in the fighter's direction. "What are you doing here?"

Hearing Louis' translation, El Tigre considered his response. How could he be quiet and still explain what he was doing? He wondered if the inspector would calm down if he said nothing.

No. "Answer me! I've seen you at too many places today for your presence to make sense. Explain!"

El Tigre considered possible answers and weighed which ones might inflame the inspector less than others. While he did this, pedestrians continued to walk around the little group as if nothing more than a friendly conversation were happening among them.

The fighter had just opened his mouth when he sniffed something. It was like the rich smell of the river, but more pungent, older, and foul. He saw a woman enter the reach of the near lamp's light as if she had simply coalesced from the darkness. She wore a dark green dress and approached from behind Inspector Hatin. Her hair was long and glistening black.

Hatin had started to bark again at El Tigre when the woman reached for the inspector's shoulder and flung him backwards into the flow of traffic. Tires screeched and horns honked. In an instant, the woman stepped forward, wrapped her arms around the big fighter, and leaped.

El Tigre felt himself go over the bridge rail backwards. The woman's eyes were a deep, almost-black green. Her breath was rank like river-bottom muck, but he forced himself to suck a long breath deep into his lungs before they struck the water.

He was a warrior. El Tigre was struggling against her grip before they had cleared the bridge railing.

Perhaps none of Legrand's other victims had fought. Perhaps they were so frightened they opened their mouths and shrunk within her grasp. Perhaps they screamed all the way to the water and, breathless, sucked the Seine into their lungs and were dead moments after entering the water. Perhaps they died of fright before they touched the river.

El Tigre fought. And the witch's eyes widened. But her arms were like metal bands.

He was a wrestler. So he wrapped his arms around the witch. In a deadly lovers' embrace, they plunged into the Seine.

Legrand was simply holding him, taking him deeper until he drowned. El Tigre squeezed—tight, tighter. The witch was light, and he could feel her bones within a thin sheath of flesh. But she was a dead creature, animated by supernatural energies, and although she appeared physically frail, her resilience was far greater than her appearance suggested. While El Tigre's efforts may have snapped the ribs of a normal human, the witch Legrand resisted his strength.

El Tigre knew the Seine's depth could reach seventeen feet. The water was murky, and he felt Legrand had carried him deeper than that.

He knew he couldn't depend on his eyes to judge exactly where he was—adrenaline charged his responses and his perception might be altered by this electricity his blood now carried. He also knew that unnatural creatures like Legrand could bend reality and fool his senses.

Yet they continued to plunge downward, he was sure of that.

His chest, expanded by the charge of air he'd taken during the fall from the bridge, ached. The witch's arms must be exceptionally long to encompass his great chest and biceps.

El Tigre released his grip and attempted to raise his arms from his shoulders to break Legrand's hold. Apparently her magic kept this attempt from working. He reached up behind her, gripped her shoulders, and pulled downward. Then he slammed his head into her nose with all the force he could muster underwater.

This blow surprised Legrand enough that she released him. In that first moment of freedom, he kicked loose and turned in the current. He shook free of his jacket and knocked off his shoes with his feet and started stroking furiously toward the surface.

The water was cold—colder than he had imagined it could be during a summery day. He kicked and swam and the darkness didn't recede. The cold intensified. El Tigre wondered if he'd confused up and down and might be heading deeper. His chest was burning. His head swirled and blood pounded in his ears. He had to reach air soon or, despite his best efforts, he would drown like Legrand's other victims.

He broke through the surface of the water. He tilted his head back and threw open his mouth and panted. He sucked in air.

Cold, fetid air.

El Tigre saw no Paris lights, no Pont Alexandre III lamps. He was still in the dark. The sounds of his gasping and splashing echoed. He was in a chamber of some sort.

Five torches snapped into flaming brightness. Arranged in a rough circle, they revealed a rocky cavern. It was roughly fifty feet across from wall to wall. El Tigre sloshed in a pool in the center of this chamber. The pool's shape mirrored that of the cavern, and a ledge about five feet wide surrounded the water on all sides.

Was this truly a cave hidden somewhere along the banks of the Seine? Or was it some magical pocket created by Legrand outside reality?

If it were a real cave, El Tigre could possibly swim back out and up to the river's surface. If it was instead some conjured place, he could easily swim away and drown, because he lacked the witch's knowledge for how to escape.

The torches mysteriously bursting into flame made him decide this was some sort of magical cavern created by Legrand, and she would probably arrive in a few minutes or even less time. What should he do?

El Tigre considered something his friend, El Puño de Bronce, told him about his excursions to what he called the Dread World. It was a foul place, a supernatural realm overseen by a creature called Mictlantecuhtli—a hideous, skeletal entity, king of the Aztec underworld. There, anarchy and chaos ruled. El Puño sought out hidden accesses to this realm and, finding them, explored its terrors to find and rescue his life's love, whom Mictlantecuhtli had kidnapped and taken there.

When El Tigre had asked El Puño how he navigated the Dread World, his fellow warrior had answered, "I don't know where I'm going. So I just keep moving."

Just keep moving. El Tigre decided that was the best advice to follow in his current situation.

He grabbed the pool's ledge and clambered out of the water. The air was cold and he was instantly chilled. He suspected the witch had no need for breathing, so he was pleased that air was available. He walked the perimeter of the cavern and found a small portal hidden in a shadow thrown by the torches. He peered in but saw nothing. He looked around the chamber once more, grabbed one of the torches from the crevice in which it had been jammed, then he ducked his head and passed through the opening.

El Tigre progressed through a narrow tunnel that looked as though it had been chiseled from the rock. He wondered if this was actually a trap laid by Legrand—would the stone walls suddenly constrict and close upon him? The hairs on the back of his neck stood up as this thought settled in his mind.

*Just keep moving.*

The tunnel was straight for twenty feet. Then it curved to the right. El Tigre reached a fork. He held the torch to one side and then the other and saw nothing that recommended one way over the other. He entered the right and continued.

After forty feet, the tunnel split into three. El Tigre's chilled wet body began to sweat. He paused only a moment, then he selected the right passage and strode in. After another forty feet, the tunnel split into four passageways. The fighter continued along the rightmost way.

This method of splitting and splitting again repeated three more times. He silently recited prayers as he moved forward into this strange labyrinth.

And then he stepped out into the cavern into which he'd originally surfaced. The floor was wet around the pool where he'd splashed out, and a torch was missing from a blackened spot where he'd removed it.

El Tigre blinked. He looked at the opening he'd just exited. It was opposite the one he'd found in a shadow, and he'd not seen this one when he first climbed out of the pool. He took a long breath, then walked to the original portal and entered it again. He retraced his steps to the first fork, then he followed the left split.

He continued taking the leftmost pathway each time he encountered a new split.

El Tigre re-entered the cavern through the same portal he'd exited previously.

"*Maldita sea.*"

So he was right: the place was a trap. Just not the sort of trap he'd thought it might be.

Something pounded in his ears as if a loud noise were rhythmically echoing within the cavern, but he heard nothing but the pool's water lapping at the surrounding stone ledges.

Then a bulge appeared in the center of the pool, and the water sloshed and Alison Legrand rose straight up and hung in the air, her shriveled feet a yard above the water's dancing surface. Ropes of water streamed from her long hair and limbs and her eyes blazed. Her mouth was wide and showed her rotten green teeth and El Tigre realized the throbbing in his ears was her laughter shaking the air—silent laughter he couldn't hear, but it shook the air and impressed his eardrums just the same in some wickedly supernatural manner.

El Tigre leaped and wrapped his arms around the witch's waist. Her body rocked like a bell clapper. The vibrations assaulting his ears changed, and he knew she was shrieking in anger. He pinioned one of her arms and swung mighty blows with his free arm. Legrand slashed at him with her talons and ripped his arm. Blood began to run.

He kicked and wrapped his legs around hers, then whipped around her until he rode her back. El Tigre shifted his arms under hers and reached until he had Legrand in a full nelson. He pressed her head forward and listened for a crack—although the witch was dead, he hoped breaking her neck would also break her power.

Legrand's arms stretched unnaturally and reached back. She clawed at El Tigre's head and shoulders.

She began to spin in the air. El Tigre clung to her. His legs were wrapped around the witch's and he continued to press her head forward.

He saw then the black scar across her neck—the sign of her execution. At that point he understood that breaking Legrand's neck would probably have no effect on the witch, if it was even possible to harm her in that way. That's when she flew backward and slammed the warrior against the cavern's rough stone wall. Stunned, he released his grip and fell to the floor. Legrand spun and dove at him. When her face was within reach, he slammed both fists upward and felt the crunch of her skull beneath his knuckles.

He could feel her screeching in pain and he covered his ears with his bruised hands.

She whipped around and a fist smashed into his head. He slid ten feet along the rocky floor. He struggled to his knees. Another blow sent him tumbling twelve feet further. He collided with something soft. El Tigre knew nothing soft was in this chamber. He wobbled to his knees again.

He saw what he'd hit.

A woman.

A dead woman. She hadn't been there earlier.

She was sitting propped against the wall. She looked about fifty years old, and her flesh was pale and wrinkled and sagged from her bones. Her green sheath dress was bedraggled and was now a size too small for her death-bloated form. Some sort of wilted weed was caught and hung from one of her dangling earrings. El Tigre figured she was one of the twelve still-missing people Inspector Hatin was looking for.

The woman's head turned. She looked at El Tigre.

Her near arm flashed out and knocked the warrior flat on his back.

His vision spun. As it settled, he scooted to a seated position, his back against the stone wall. He looked around.

All twelve missing persons sat around the pool. They hadn't been there when he'd first arrived. They stared at him.

They were all dead.

Legrand floated in the air over the pool. Her mouth moved, and the animated corpses stood and began walking toward El Tigre.

Using the wall for support, El Tigre pushed to his feet.

The twelve dead people didn't turn their singular gaze away from him.

Another little prayer ran through El Tigre's head. He looked at the dead eyes staring at him. He had no wish to harm these corpses, but he felt sure Legrand would soon have them attack him. Yet he knew the souls that once had inhabited these bodies had fled these human shells when the witch had murdered them. Now they were no longer people. They were Legrand's puppets.

El Tigre whispered, "May God forgive me."

At some silent signal, the corpses charged El Tigre.

Six raced toward him from one direction around the pool, and six came the other direction.

El Tigre faced those approaching from his right. He stepped close to the wall as the first got within reach and shoved the dead woman hard toward the pool. She staggered, lost her balance, and toppled into the water.

El Tigre spun and met the dead man coming from behind him. He grabbed the corpse's shoulder and left side of its head and smashed it against the stone wall. He felt the skull crush on impact, heard bones in its arm and shoulder snap. The warrior flung the body away from him, toward the pool.

He spun again. This time El Tigre encountered a sharp blow to his belly from a hard first. The warrior gasped and took a step back. The dead woman who'd struck him pulled back her fist for another blow.

As she did so, El Tigre lunged forward and hooked his right fist into her face. Her jaw broke and the corpse staggered. He swiped his left forearm into her ribs. The animated puppet somersaulted into the water.

El Tigre felt a terrific kidney chop that dropped him to his knees. The pain ran through his torso and he groaned. He focused on one thought: He had to get to his feet before the remaining corpses mobbed him. Nine of the twelve were left.

He pushed upward and rammed his head into the gut of the creature before him so that it was knocked back and crashed into the two behind it. They collapsed to the stone floor and the last of the six attacking from that side tripped and fell over the three before it.

El Tigre extricated himself from the tangle, and then kicked tremendous blows at the squirming bodies until all four were on the edge of the pool and on the verge of tumbling into it.

Five corpses remained behind him. El Tigre wasted only a moment on thought. Despite the awful pain from the blow over his kidney, he reached down and snatched a necklace of thick silver links from one of the women at his feet. He wrapped it around his left fist, then he used the moaning forms at the edge of the pool as a springboard and launched himself at Legrand.

He clutched her waist and climbed up as they hung in the air above the pool. The witch thrashed in his grip. She clawed at his face and arms as he pounded her with his chain-wrapped fist. Silver supposedly worked against vampires and werewolves, he'd been told. What about dead witches?

It seemed to have no effect—at least nothing so dramatic as he'd been hoping, based on the bad movies he'd watched. His blows dented Legrand's face and body, but the depressions would fill in nearly immediately. No sign remained of the head-butt he'd given her earlier. Meanwhile, sharp pains crossed his back, and her talons drew fiery lines where they ripped his flesh. His hand throbbed as the necklace links dug into his fingers and knuckles. The witch's silent shrieks threatened to burst his eardrums.

El Tigre gritted his teeth and continued punching.

Legrand dropped from the air suddenly and splashed into the pool. She wrapped her lengthening arms around the warrior and plunged ever deeper into the black water's depths.

El Tigre wriggled and wrestled and thumped Legrand's head and body, but he couldn't free himself. He'd managed to suck down a quick breath before hitting the water, but he knew it wouldn't be enough.

Down, down they went. El Tigre's struggles grew weaker as the water temperature fell. Legrand's iron-like arms tightened. The warrior's chest burned as he held his air and his chest felt near to bursting. Black globs began to fill his vision. A high-pitched squeal grew louder in his ears.

He noticed, somehow, their descent had stopped. They hung in the cold water. Legrand's grip had loosened around his trunk. She thrashed against him and jarred bubbles from his mouth. He was ready to slip away into a new, deeper darkness.

Then El Tigre saw a faint light. A pale blueness filled his sight and expelled the black blobs. No longer able to hold his breath, he exhaled and his lungs drew in deeply—instead of sucking in the foul water he'd expected, he tasted air.

As his vision cleared, he saw a surprising sight: He and the witch were surrounded by a single large bubble of blue light.

Legrand flung El Tigre away and he settled softly, like a falling feather, on the bottom of the globe. He watched as the witch twisted and flailed against an invisible opponent. Her screams, still silent but evident, no longer tortured his ears.

El Tigre didn't know what was happening. Had he lost enough oxygen that he was now delirious? Was he drowning and not coherent enough to realize it was happening?

Then a hand reached into the bubble, followed by a wrist. It came through the bubble from outside without bursting the globe of blue light and air. El Tigre held his breath when he saw that the hand and its wrist were formed of water that flowed within the shape of the hand.

The hand was massive. It reached into the bubble and grasped Alison Legrand. Only her head and shoulders and feet were exposed above and below the fist that held her. The witch's eyes widened and her mouth opened so that El Tigre could see every one of her teeth. Then the giant hand pulled Legrand out of the blue bubble with a little burp of noise.

El Tigre put his face against the wall of the bubble so he could see through the strange membrane. He was careful not to push too hard—he didn't want to fall through the membrane into the water outside. But he could see through the pale blue wall and could make out what was happening there.

The giant hand clutching Legrand belonged to a giant woman. She was pale blue, like the globe holding El Tigre, and she was made of water—water that somehow held its shape and was different from the surrounding black currents. Her long fluid locks flowed from her head and her blue robes streamed about her amazon-like body.

Legrand's jaws champed and black tendrils swam from her mouth, but these inky extrusions broke apart and were carried past the giant woman.

El Tigre remembered Marie Dupont's words about the goddess of the Seine: Sequana.

As he watched, the giant Sequana brought Legrand toward her face. As she did so, her features changed. Her blue hair and robes flowed away and her body moved into a different form. Her eyes flared with a bright green light that made El Tigre squint. Her jaws opened and her skull extended and lengthened more like that of a swimming creature. Her open mouth revealed concentric rows of sharp, triangular teeth. Her watery flesh shifted and her appearance was completely different, completely inhuman.

She pushed the struggling Legrand into her mouth and gobbled the witch down.

El Tigre turned away. He couldn't watch any more of that. What would this chthonic deity now do with him?

The blue bubble must have started floating upward without El Tigre noticing, because it surfaced in the middle of the pool in the witch's cavern.

All twelve dead people were out of the water. No longer animated by Legrand, they lay strewn around the chamber's stone floor.

The blue bubble bobbed on the water's surface several moments before floating to the edge of the pool. When it nudged the ledge surround the water and stayed in place, El Tigre decided this was a sign for him to leave the bubble. He crawled to that side of the sphere and pushed against its wall. His hand and arm went through the membrane with a tingle passing along his limb.

He soon stood on the ledge with the corpses.

The blue bubble evaporated into wisps of mist that floated to the ceiling and dispersed.

El Tigre looked around at his bloated companions. "Now what?" he asked the raw stone walls.

The water in the pool started burbling, then roiling. Its surface swelled upward, and then a large, ungainly shape burst through and flung spray throughout the cavern.

It was a massive duck, the size of a dinghy. It shook its head and wings before settling down to floating on the water. El Tigre had stepped away from the pool and his back pressed against the rocky wall. The duck moved its sleek head this way and that. Its coloration matched that of no duck El Tigre had ever seen. The keratin of its long, wide beak was incised with curving lines and dots—combinations that in some ways resembled paisley. If they pictured something, the warrior couldn't make it out, so he imagined they were ornamental or magical symbols. El Tigre saw his reflection in the large black eye the bird turned his way.

*"Hola Señor Pato."*

The duck continued to examine El Tigre for a few minutes. Then, quick as a cat, it opened its bill and extended its neck and swallowed the warrior in a single gulp.


CHAPTER EIGHT

A police squad cordoned both ends of Pont Alexandre III.

The Seine below the bridge was busy with police boats shining sharp beams of light into the water, with divers surfacing and diving.

On one of the boats, Inspector Hugo Hatin was directing the work while drinking cup after paper cup of black coffee and chain smoking cigarettes.

On the right bank, among the gawkers who remained at four in the morning, stood Marie Dupont and Louis D'Arnot. Worry and waiting had drained their faces of vitality. They had watched the furious activities of the police and the underwater rescue and recovery squads for hours. Because of what they'd learned during their research before El Tigre was snatched away, they'd held little hope these efforts would prove successful. As the night passed into the lightening dark of the morning, what hope remained had dwindled to despair.

"The priest was right," Louis had whispered at some point after midnight.

"Shut up!" ordered Marie. A moment later, she reached out and held his hand.

The reporter expected Hatin to call off the search at any time. The boats were holding up river traffic, and morning rush hour would require the bridge to open.

Standing with the small crowd and surrounded by its exhalations of stale wine breath, cigarette smoke, and general unwashed body funk, Marie was close to giving up this vigil. Perhaps she could push her hopes until dawn broke. Perhaps she could only last a half hour more. Perhaps she would give up when the trembling old man beside her finished his smoke.

Baffled by what she had heard and seen during the day, distressed still by the suddenness of the attack and her inability to react in time to do—what?—something to stop the violence, and feeling the weight of guilt for her helplessness and for her complete expectation that all this churning in the river would prove worthless, Marie clenched her jaws and tightened her fists in angry defiance of the lead weight in her head and belly.

Then she released the tension and her shoulders slumped.

When someone to her left called out, "*Regardez là!*" her tired mind and body didn't react immediately. Then she heard Louis' sudden intake of breath. She moved her head and looked.

An odd shape was drawing closer out of the darkness from the direction of the Île de la Cité. Marie squinted her aching eyes as Louis clutched her elbow. What in the world could that possibly be?

It was a boat.

A black boat—no, where the many artificial lights touched it, a pale blue gleam showed. It appeared to drift, as it had no sail nor engine.

It was shaped like a giant duck. Its prow rose up in an elegant curve of a neck that ended in a duck's head and wide bill. By squinting, Marie could see wiggling symbols carved on the beak.

Standing on the boat's deck was the wide-shouldered El Tigre Azul.

The boat shifted from the center of the river toward the right bank. It slipped up to the quai and docked near an ambulance waiting for the police boats to find something.

The ambulance team helped El Tigre to shore as Marie and Louis ran up. The reporter glanced at the boat. She saw no obvious rudder or way of piloting the big duck. She grabbed El Tigre's near arm. "Are you all right? How did you get here?"

He started to answer but Louis slammed into him and embraced the warrior. He kissed both his cheeks and hugged him again.

El Tigre patted the interpreter's shoulder. "Louis, that hurts."

"*Oh je suis désolé. Pardon, désolé.*" Louis backed away, abashed.

El Tigre's shirt and trousers hung in blood-stained shreds. His mask was torn. He was barefoot. As he was being led to the ambulance, he directed one of the ambulance techs to the boat. "The bodies are there."

Louis stared a moment before he translated for the ambulance team.

Marie stood nearby while El Tigre's wounds were tended. "What happened?"

The masked man took a long breath and exhaled it before answering. He was clearly exhausted. "That is a long, strange story. And then a duck swallowed me. Everything turned black. When I woke up, I was on the river." He grinned. "Inspector Hatin isn't going to like that story, is he?"

Marie shook her head. "His hero is not Inspector Maigret."

More ambulances were arriving to take the bodies that were being removed from the boat.

The reporter looked at the police boats under the bridge. "Once he sees all the activity over here, he'll probably want to join in."

Hearing this, El Tigre conferred with Louis. Marie watched the last body being carried off the boat. Once it was empty, the duck-headed craft pulled away from the quai and turned upstream. No one was aboard. It was twenty yards away when Marie noticed it was sinking into the water. Quickly.

In five minutes, it was gone, underwater.

Marie was staring at the place the boat had disappeared when El Tigre and Louis joined her. "It's gone," she said. "Who was piloting that weird boat?"

"Weird boat," El Tigre said. "That says it all."

"What?"

El Tigre gestured away from all the excitement. "Where can we get breakfast?"

Marie was having trouble following the conversation. "Breakfast?"

"I told Louis to tell the ambulance driver to tell the cops we'll go to headquarters in a couple of hours to give a statement to Inspector Hatin." El Tigre shook his head. "I'll need some food to get through that. And maybe a change of clothes."

Marie gave a last glance at the Seine, but there was no sign of the duck boat. "That is definitely true."

The trio walked away from the flashing lights and stayed clear of the ambulances rushing away. El Tigre was limping slightly. "It's been a long night."

"That's true too," Marie agreed. "And I still haven't interviewed you for *L'Équipe*."

"*Si*. Excellent," El Tigre said. "My day is planned out before the sun is up."

After breakfast, he would see Inspector Hatin to give his statement and answer questions, and he would finally get to see the recesses of 36 Quai des Orfèvres.

El Tigre Azul smiled. Things were looking up.

.

# { 3 }

# A Witch in Time

*Una Brujo en el Tiempo*

*The Pleistocene – The Valley of Mexico*

The breeze skipped across the lake filling the Valley of Mexico and climbed the slopes of the surrounding hills and stirred the grasses growing there, bowing and sweeping their green strands in graceful dances. The air was full with the aromas of warm water and the blossoms that bobbed their heads. The water's surface was fretted by the playful wind so that the ribbons and curls of light that flashed and danced on the water seemed to kick the low waves into movement.

The songs of birds and the whir of wing feathers and the snicks and burrs of insects lent a piquant vitality to the day. Far to the north the land was covered with ice. Here, life was golden and each breath was a song. Day followed night followed day, and the sun warmed this world and the stars cooled it. Motes of pollen floated and flew. The tongues of the lake lapped against the shoulders of the hills. Clouds began to flock together in the east. Another shower of rain would pass through during the coming night and stipple the lake. Seeds would sprout under the sun's caress the following day.

Breath Of The Wind hummed as it combed through the grasses and the leaves of the trees that stood atop the hills. This life was glorious.

*1974 – Monterrey, Cadereyta Jiménez, Montemorelos*

When El Tigre Azul woke up in Monterrey he expected to enjoy a leisurely drive to Montemorelos, about an hour and a half away. Then he would rest awhile before preparing for the match he would fight that night at a high school gymnasium.

His plans were thwarted as he placed his bag into the trunk of his car. It was a 1972 Dodge Charger. Its blue paint shone in the sun like a jewel's surface. He'd spent the night at the home of a friend who'd retired from wrestling and now ran a school for luchadores. As El Tigre shut the trunk lid, one of his friend's daughters ran out of the house shouting his name.

"What is it, Perla?"

"*El telefono*. You have a call."

El Tigre followed her back into the house and picked up the phone. The caller was Ramon, his manager.

"*Buenos días*, Tiger! Why aren't you on the road?"

El Tigre sighed. "I was just leaving."

"*Excelente*! That gives you time to pick up Arturo."

"Arturo?"

"Arturo Moreno, you know him."

El Tigre paused before responding. "Arturo Moreno, the luchador?"

"*Si*."

"Arturo Moreno, the luchador I'm fighting tonight? I'm supposed to give him a ride?"

Even Ramon couldn't entirely ignore the heat in El Tigre's voice. But he responded again with his typical confidence. "*Si.*"

Ramon could detect El Tigre's exasperation swimming through the silence that filled the phone line. After a few moments, the fighter asked, "Where is he?"

"Cadereyta Jiménez."

"That's at least half an hour out of my way. Nearly an hour!"

It was as if El Tigre could hear Ramon's shrug as his voice came out of the receiver: "He needs a ride, you're both going to the same place. If he doesn't show up, there won't be a fight, and many of your most faithful fans will be so disappointed."

El Tigre didn't listen to the radio, nor did he sing while he drove southeast through Juarez and on through scrubby farmland to Cadereyta Jiménez, a smaller city than Monterrey. Only the growl and rumble of the Charger's V8 engine accompanied his wandering thoughts. The peaks of the Sierra Madre Oriental range were visible to the west. El Tigre glanced that direction occasionally. He thought about getting away from Ramon and lucha libre for a time and going up into the mountains. The thought of Ramon made him shake his head. The pleasant images of trekking through the mountains disappeared. El Tigre traveled in a guayabera and a comfortable pair of chinos, but his dissatisfaction with the day's progress made his clothes feel tight.

Arturo Moreno was very polite and thanked El Tigre very sincerely as the two men climbed into the blue muscle car. The passenger mentioned how sharp-looking the Dodge Charger was. "Nice lines. The rear looks kind of lifted up, like the lower front end is ready to eat up the road." El Tigre answered with only a few syllables. Even though his driver wore a mask, Arturo could tell El Tigre was unhappy.

Arturo didn't wear a mask. Just thinking about wearing a mask—even just to try one on—made his face itch. He scratched his thick black eyebrows with his knuckles. "Hey, I'm sorry about needing a ride."

El Tigre shrugged. "It's not your fault. I'm just angry at Ramon."

Arturo uttered a curt bark of laughter. "Yeah, Ramon: *la joda.*"

Both men laughed. The trip got better after that.

The rest of the day went well. They drove south for an hour and then turned onto the main highway southeast to Montemorelos. Once there, they settled in, had a meal, and went to the high school to get ready for their match.

By the time the fights began, the gym was crowded. The two opening matches featured local luchadores and warmed up the spectators nicely. Fans for both El Tigre and Arturo Moreno were in the building, and they called out the fighters' names with great energy.

Both men fought well. The fans were thrilled with the performance. Arturo won, but El Tigre was satisfied with the way the fight had gone. The luchadores waved to the crowd as they left the ring. The spectators' chatter was lively as they filed out of the building. As they left the bright lights of the gymnasium and stepped into the night, exhilaration climbed the ladders of their ribs and the children scampered and the adults laughed, young and old.

After cleaning up and dressing in street clothes, the two fighters left the gym and dropped into the Dodge's seats. Exhaustion wrapped around their shoulders. El Tigre drove to find a taqueria before they headed to their hotel.

They were coming alongside a station just as a bus turned from the street to stop along the platform. At the same time half a dozen youths—either older teenagers or young men and women barely entering their twenties—dashed from the station across the street in front of El Tigre.

He stomped the brakes. As the Dodge stopped with a squeal and a jerk, Arturo shouted, "Hey! Watch out!"

The last of the youths made a rude gesture at the car's occupants as he trotted out of the street. El Tigre pushed the horn rim half-circling the steering wheel to toot his irritation at the young people.

No one heard the horn.

The sound was lost in an explosion at the bus station.

The car rocked as El Tigre raced away and turned into a side street to avoid falling debris.

The engine hardly had a moment to completely stop before both men had exited the Dodge and stared at the fireball climbing the sky across the street. They watched as timbers and bricks tumbled from overhead and rolled across the pavement toward them. Once everything blown into the sky had landed, the two fighters ran toward the burning station.

The bus that had just arrived lay on its side. Its green and white and silver finishes were scorched and its windows were smashed. Groans, screams, and weeping could be heard from the people inside. After the luchadores forced open the door, El Tigre climbed into the bus. The driver was dead. El Tigre began handing out the injured passengers to Arturo, who carried them one by one across the street to the opposite curb. By this time a crowd had gathered. Arturo pointed at a few to start tending to the wounded people he brought out. He directed others to help him carry passengers from the bus.

Fire sirens and ambulance horns were soon howling. When the engines arrived, the luchadores had more help. While they moved people, hoses were attached and jets of water attacked the flames working over the station building. Steam clouded the air and made seeing difficult.

Once the fires were out, smoke still rose from the broken building. The bitter smell of ashes filled the air. The exhausted luchadores circled the station. Their clothes were torn and wet and stained with blood and soot. They shook their heads and staggered a little bit. They shook hands with firemen and exchanged encouraging words.

They'd reached the side of the station that faced the street on which El Tigre had parked the Dodge. This was the only wall of the building still standing. It was covered with green tiles whose glaze was cracked and soot-smudged and shimmering with water that still ran from the ruined roof. El Tigre pointed. "Look at that."

Arturo looked at the wall. "*Qué?*"

"The last thing intact." El Tigre waved at the green tiles. "No *pintada*—the station workers do a good job of cleaning off any graffiti. But right there, just that little squiggle."

The pair walked closer to the wall to study the marking. Arturo scowled. "It's a—what is it? A badly drawn 'B'?" He turned to El Tigre. "What's it mean?"

"I don't know."

Arturo ran both hands through his dirty curls and scrubbed the top of his head. "You think those kids did it? The ones who ran across the street?"

El Tigre shrugged. "Maybe."

"You think they did all this? Blew up the place?"

"I don't know. Why would they do that?"

Arturo made a strangled noise in his throat. "Who knows? I'm too tired to think."

"Come on." El Tigre led the way to the parked Dodge. "Let's get to our beds before the roosters wake us up."


*The late Pleistocene – The Valley of Mexico*

The voice of insects—sawing legs, whirring wings, clicking wing sheaths—pulsed in counterpoint to the shifting rustle of grass and upright stalks of *teosinte* stirred by Breath Of The Wind. In another day or two, a storm would blow in from the gulf that lay to the east, and the lake in the valley would turn the color of lead and Breath Of The Wind would replace today's music with moaning and groaning. After a few more days and the sun's drying, the hiss and slither of grass blades' caressing would return.

The two-legged animals had been drifting toward the Valley of Mexico from the cold north. Their advance had been slow. They followed the animals for their hunting, moving from one camp to another over time as the population of their prey thinned and left for other territories. They flung stones that flew like the birds they brought down and ate. They settled for a time, gathering fruit and seeds and hunting what was available, then they gathered what little they carried and moved elsewhere. They shifted and flowed from place to place with the animals and the flowering and fruiting of plants just like the seasons rolled through their reliable dance.

Breath Of The Wind watched them and ran through their camps. The two-legged animals were so different from what had been there before—mastodon, horse, mammoth, antelope, dire wolf, and the smaller mammals and birds—but their habits were very like the other animals that drifted here and there with the rains and the dry season. Breath Of The Wind didn't mind the new animals. They were simply different.


## 1974 – Chapultepec, Mexico City

El Tigre Azul stood at 2,325 meters above sea level and took in the view. The terrace gardens of Castillo de Chapultepec lay before him, and the Mexico City skyline stretched beyond that.

He stood on one of the castle's galleries and enjoyed the scene. He'd been invited here to capture a ghost. All he'd found was a tour guide who belched a lot. So pausing for a long look was a pleasant diversion.

It was quite possible the castle had a ghost. Maybe more than one. After all, the construction had taken eighty years, beginning in 1785. The number of regime changes, battles and wars during that time likely would've resulted in at least a few ghosts. Supposedly the hill on which the castle stood had been a sacred place for the Aztecs. El Tigre wouldn't have been surprised if a few unhappy Nahuatl-speaking spirits liked to rattle the glassware.

The dyspeptic showed up and told El Tigre he had a phone call. He led the luchador to a small office, where a young women handed a phone's receiver to him as he entered. "*Hola?*"

The caller identified himself as the director of Bosque de Cha-pultepec, the massive park within which the castle stood. He'd heard El Tigre Azul was in the park, and he needed the luchador's help.

"In what way?" El Tigre asked.

"The zoo animals are getting loose!"

After a pause: "*Qué?*"

"The zoo! The animals! They're running loose!"

El Tigre thought of some fights he'd had in the ring with El Toro, El Jaguar de Jade, El Cóndor Llameante, even Dr. Zaius. "What do you want me to do?"

"Stop the people letting them loose!"

"Oh. Okay."

El Tigre hustled to his car, parked outside the castle. The Bosque de Chapultepec was a massive park, one of the largest in the western hem-isphere. It would take only about five minutes to drive to the zoo, which lay on the park's northwestern corner.

Once he arrived and parked the Dodge, El Tigre charged through the crowds still streaming out of the gate. Parents carried children, *niñas* and *niños* ran and yammered, young men and women in zoo uniforms trotted along and clutched their cameras to their chests.

As El Tigre moved deeper into the zoo, the number of terror-stricken runners thinned to just a dozen or so widely separated couples and single visitors. He headed to the pathway leading to the right, where most of the crowd had come from.

He scanned the grounds for anyone who appeared to be freeing animals from their enclosures. He knew anyone who'd done so could have fled with the legitimate visitors, but if it was possible to stop someone from releasing any more animals, he was willing to try.

El Tigre also kept an eye open for any beasts that might decide to stalk him. "I'm just a visiting tiger," he whispered. "Please don't bite me."

He hoped the animals were well-fed enough to have no interest in chasing a man in a luchador mask. He also thought the strangeness of being out of their usual settings might make the beasts anxious and incite them to attack anyone they encountered. Sirens were approaching the zoo from different directions. Knowing professionals were arriving to herd the animals relieved some of worry making El Tigre's back and shoulders tight.

His anxiety returned when he felt the vibrations of an explosion through his feet. A cloud of dust and smoke rose in the distance, and El Tigre judged it was near or at one of the zoo's entrance gates.

A high squeal—perhaps from a boar or wart hog?—followed by an elephant's trumpeting let him know the animals were truly alarmed now. He was deciding to return to the gate through which he'd entered the zoo's gardens when he heard the sound of galloping approach from a bend in the path. El Tigre quickly dodged behind the thick bole of a tall tree. He stood in place and held his breath and saw a white rhinoceros rush past and trailing a swirling cloud of dust.

"Whew."

A charging rhino was nothing to fool around with. And there were more ferocious creatures in the zoo. El Tigre knew he now had no chance of tracking down the people creating this terror. He needed to get out of the gardens. Quickly.

He hurried back along the path he'd followed, staying close to the edge in case he needed to hide in the shrubbery and trees that grew along its sides, when another explosion shook the ground and the air. This one came from a different direction. He guessed it was the site of another gate.

Apparently releasing the animals was just the first step. Whoever was behind this mayhem wanted the freed animals driven out of the zoo and roaming the wider environs of the park and perhaps even the city streets.

El Tigre ran faster. He knew the explosions would frighten the animals and drive them away from the noise and shock—which meant they could be heading his direction. He needed to be outside the zoo before they caught up with him.

Would the bomb bursts frighten the animals so much they would ignore him if he encountered them? Or would their fright make them lash out at anyone they met on their way to escaping the thundering blasts?

Leaves wheeled down from overhead. The tree canopy rattled as terrified monkeys raced through the branches howling and screeching. Two elephants thumped rapidly behind El Tigre, and he dove into the shrubbery by the path to let them pass. He lay on the loam and raised up on an elbow. He was face-to-face with a young boy. The child, perhaps four years old, stared at the luchador with wide eyes that swam in tears. His lips were clamped on the fingers of one hand, and the other hand wound circles in the dark hair over his ear.

El Tigre got to his knees. "*Hola, pequeño.* My name is El Tigre Azul. What about your name?"

The boy just stared.

"Looking for mama?"

The child ducked his head a little and looked up through his lashes at El Tigre.

The luchador lifted the boy in his arms and stood. "Let's get you out of here." He looked past the shrubbery at the path. "Let's get both of us out of here."

El Tigre headed toward the gate at a steady trot. He took care not to jostle the child so much that he would be even more frightened. They finally reached the large open-air concourse where the zoo's paths intersected before the entrance gate. At the same moment, a Siberian tiger bounded into the area from the opposite path. Fully ten feet long from nose to tail tip, the beast halted when it spotted the luchador and the boy.

El Tigre stopped as well.

Luchador and tiger stared at each other. The giant feline showed its teeth. Its tail whipped from side to side. The tiger lowered its body close to the ground and oozed forward. When it stopped, it crouched and looked ready to pounce.

The boy started to whimper. El Tigre stroked the child's hair and weighed his chances for running to the gate or back into the path.

He decided the odds were bad, no matter which direction he decided to go.

The tiger leaped.

El Tigre ducked and rushed toward the tiger as it flew into the air.

The zoo gate exploded.

El Tigre had meant to run under the arc of the tiger's leap. Instead, he and the boy and the beast were blown head over heels into the thick shrubs that divided the paths leading away from the concourse. El Tigre heard the tiger screech as it tumbled into the foliage. That's all he heard for several minutes. The explosion had blown the hearing from his ears.

El Tigre felt vibrations through the soil pressing against his back. He guessed those came from the tiger scrambling up and rushing away in terror. He also felt the child squirming and heaving within his arms. Apparently the luchador's body had shielded the boy from most of the blast's force—El Tigre's limbs certainly ached as though they'd caught a fair share of the blow.

He moved slowly and made calming noises to the boy. On his knees, El Tigre moved around and made sure nothing was broken before he clambered to his feet. Once again he peered into the path before he stepped out and staggered to the entrance.

Broken stone, shattered tiles, twisted metal lay everywhere. A cloud of dust and smoke hung in the air like fog.

He stumbled over the debris and beyond the ruins of the gate. Someone approached through the cloud and took his arm, and another figure appeared and took the child from his grasp. They led El Tigre several yards before helping him to sit on the pavement and lean against the side of an automobile. He noticed the car's tires were flat and a deep dent marked the driver's door. His helpers disappeared into the smoke. El Tigre closed his eyes and breathed slowly and waited for the ringing in his skull to diminish.

As his hearing returned, he heard a ticking. It finally resolved into the sound of someone clapping. El Tigre got to his feet and walked through the thinning cloud toward the sound's source.

It was a woman. She stood between two wrecked cars and clapped her hands. El Tigre stood and watched a few moments before he said, "Are you okay?"

"No, I'm a wreck," she answered. Anger made her words sharp. "A wreck just like these cars. We're all wrecks. You, too." She'd stopped clapping.

El Tigre heard sirens approaching. He glanced around, hoping to spot an ambulance, because he thought this woman might need one. "What do you mean?"

"When people act like animals, the true animals should be running free." She shook a finger in the direction of the ruined gate. "Not caged up like they are lesser creatures than the monsters running the world, wrecking us."

El Tigre studied the woman. She was about forty years old and wore big sunglasses, an over-large, sunflower-yellow tee shirt, poppy-red capri pants and dirty sneakers. "Did you let the animals out?"

"Don't be ridiculous!" she scoffed. "But why wouldn't I?" She whipped around and looked at him. He could detect her fierce scowl even behind the large glasses. "My oldest son—the government killed him in the plaza at Tlatelolco. In the last year, my younger son disappeared. My daughter disappeared. My grandson disappeared!" She wailed this last. "There's a dark war being waged against us! They don't declare themselves, just steal away our children in the night!"

She whipped out a hand and clutched one tattered lapel of his ruined jacket. "The beasts are killing us. It's better to let the true animals free."

She released his coat before turning and stalking away. As she'd had hold of him, El Tigre had seen clearly the drawing on her tee shirt. It was a symbol he now recognized: a scrawled B, like the one he'd seen on the bombed bus station.

He didn't know much about it, but he'd learned a group of people were using it as a sign of their discontent.

Just as they were using bombs and acts of defiance, like setting the zoo animals free.

Fire engines and ambulances and police cars had screeched into place and disgorged their occupants, who'd scattered and herded and tended people and animals alike. What remained of the floating dust and smoke still reflected the emergency vehicles' flashing lights and, in the dimming day, created the atmosphere of a grim circus.

El Tigre made his way to what remained of the gate. A section of stone wall remained standing. Scrawled on the wall in thick black paint were these words:

*Saltamontes Cerro*

"Grasshopper Hill"—the translation of the old Nahuatl word used by the Aztecs: *Chapultepec.*


## *1800 BC*

The two-legged animals grew more numerous. They reproduced like the other animals and gave birth and many of the helpless young ones died, just as was true for the other animals. Still, the numbers of the two-legged animals increased. As more of them survived, and as more appeared from the north, many of their little bands moved farther south.

The novelty they presented attracted Breath Of The Wind's attention. Their habits slowly changed. Instead of bands numbering eight or ten at the most, they were now huddling in larger groups.

Time passed. The two-legged animals were still nomads, but their paths did not drift like seed upon the wind as they once did. Now following the seasons, their travels were circumscribed within certain revisited and familiar sites. The bands who herded together continued to grow larger.

As they traveled less frequently, Breath Of The Wind noticed why. Their herds collected seeds and planted them. They would not move while waiting for the seeds to sprout and grow. The two-legged animals relied on their foraging less than when they first appeared from the north. They harvested the plants they grew. More of the younglings survived longer.

The rest of the world continued as it had always done in Breath Of The Wind's memory. Plants grew, seeds flew and found a place and flourished or died. The rains came, the season of blazing sun approached and withdrew. Everything was as it was. Everything except the two-legged animals. They changed how they acted, and they changed the world within their reach.

This changing disturbed Breath Of The Wind.

### *1974 – Coatzacoalcos, Veracruz, Mexico*

El Tigre Azul wished he were still standing on the beach with the city of Coatzacoalcos at his back while he stared north at the waves washing in over the Gulf of Mexico. Even with the unceasing sounds of shipping carried over the water from the nearby port at the Coatzacoalcos River, the sight of the waves and the delicate touch of the breezes had been very relaxing.

When his work was done, he could return to the beach. Until then, he was tracking down a meeting site for a group whose members called themselves *mariposas*.

El Tigre had learned the group's name while investigating the hand-drawn symbol he'd seen marked here and there in various Mexican cities, particularly where acts of violent defiance had occurred. He'd noticed the scrawled B at the bombed bus station in Montemorelos and at the zoo in Mexico City.

He'd found out the symbol wasn't a B: It was a butterfly's wing.

So, butterfly's wing, *mariposas*.

El Tigre had come to Coatzacoalcos on the trail of a bank robber. He'd learned from a cop in Tuxtla Gutiérrez the thief had a tremendous fondness for *galletas*. After arriving in Coatzacoalcos, El Tigre had checked one bakery after another until he spotted his quarry leaving one and licking his fingers while carrying an open paper bag filled with cookies. That's when El Tigre nabbed him.

Afterward, while talking about the robber with a newspaper reporter who claimed without a smile his name was Juan Gaceta, the writer had mentioned the troubles El Tigre had encountered elsewhere with *Las Mariposas*. The group—the writer called them a *culto*—had stirred up some grief in Coatzacoalcos, but nothing like he'd read about happening elsewhere.

"The first ones came here from La Venta, about sixty kilometers away," the reporter said. "That's the story, anyway. They deface buildings, they stop traffic by sitting down in a street—nuisances, really. Not much else."

The writer had told him the rumor about *Las Mariposas'* meeting place.

El Tigre drove his blue Dodge Charger to the address the reporter gave him. He cruised past a brick building painted white with a large sign on its side: *Banco Nacional de Mexico*. It sat on one corner of an intersection. Parked before it were a blue Volkswagen, a red Mustang, a yellow Volkswagen, and, at the end of the sidewalk, a burro was tied to a street sign's pole.

El Tigre turned the corner and parked in front of the bank's side door.

He went back to the burro and scratched its nose. The beast rolled its eyes at him as if it were tired of strangers' attentions.

Seemingly rebuffed for his kindness, the luchador approached the empty storefront adjoining the bank building. Dust layered the shop's windows. Sheets of butcher paper had been taped to their inside surfaces and some had fallen loose. Looking through these gaps, El Tigre saw a few empty display cases and scattered sheets of newspaper. Between the storefront and the bank was a door El Tigre opened to reveal an ascending staircase. According to Gaceta, *Las Mariposas* met in the rooms above the store.

El Tigre stepped in and closed the door. He listened several moments, but heard nothing from upstairs. He climbed, moving slowly and quietly.

The room at the top was completely open. No walls interrupted the view from the front of the building to the back. The windows at each end of this expanse were covered with thin canvas tarpaulins. They glowed in the day's light. The light suddenly changed when the tarps billowed where missing window panes allowed a breeze to enter. Through the room's strange dusk, El Tigre saw something crawling across the walls.

Cautioned by a career of weird encounters, El Tigre approached the nearest wall. It was covered with photographs taped to its surface. Some were clipped from magazines. Others were snapshots. What his gaze had interpreted as something crawling had actually been the loose corners moving in the breeze.

He walked around the room. All four walls were covered in this fashion.

No people were framed within these photographs. Only scenes from nature were pictured: flowers, trees, insects, animals, landscapes. Nothing domesticated. Every photo had been shot in natural environments.

No sign of human existence was captured: no cars, buildings, fences, power lines or poles.

El Tigre looked up.

The ceiling was likewise covered. These photos all showed different scenes of the star-crowded night sky and the moon in various phases.

Something caught his attention on the floor. He moved aside a tarp curtaining a window to let in more light. A giant scrawled B—a butter-fly's wing—had been drawn on the floor with black spray paint. The reporter had been right: *Las Mariposas.*

El Tigre noticed also a rectangular hatch cut into the floor's planks. He could see a small splintered area along its edge where a knife or screwdriver had been used repeatedly to lever up the door from the opening it covered. He squeezed his fingertips into the gap and lifted the hatch. The shop's back storeroom, cluttered with trash, tangles of wire and torn-open boxes, lay below. A ladder was propped against the edge of the hatchway. El Tigre shimmied through the opening and clambered down.

At the bottom of the ladder, El Tigre saw a curtained doorway that led to the front of the store, a wooden door in the back wall that he figured was an exit outside, and an open set of steps that descended to a basement.

He had taken a single step toward the stairs when he blacked out.

When El Tigre was again aware of what was happening, a high whine circled the inside of his skull. The whine resolved into a cacoph-ony of sirens. He opened his eyes and found a uniformed policeman was helping him to his feet.

He looked around. He was standing in a parking lot adjoining an alley. Cars were turned on their sides or were completely flipped onto their hoods. "What happened?"

"*Una bomba*," the cop said. He had a hard grip on the luchador's arm to keep him steady.

El Tigre blinked. He saw the remains of the store. Half of it was gone.

The bank wasn't a building any longer. It was a pile of rubble. Thick cables of dust and black smoke twined upward and wove a pall in the sky.

He took a step and lost his balance. The cop kept him upright. El Tigre saw a door under his feet. He'd been blown out the back of the storeroom when the bomb exploded.

*Las Mariposas*, he thought.

When El Tigre was able to walk without assistance, and after he'd given his statement to the police, he returned to where he'd parked his car. The burro was gone. The blue Dodge Charger was flattened under the side wall of the bank.

### 1750 BC

Butterfly Wing was returning to the village. He carried three birds he'd brought down today. Two had been perched on tree branches when his dart points knocked them off their horny feet to tumble to the ground. The other was on the wing when he skewered it in the sky!

He didn't walk too quickly, because he stopped occasionally to look at the birds and admire their bright plumage. A bright red feather from the largest—the color of life's flow—would make a fine present to give Pink Flower In The Rain. He imagined how she might wear his gift— because of course she would accept it—and thought she might braid it into her hair. Or hang from her wrist. No, she was too careful in her work, and a feather hanging from her wrist would drag through the ground *teosinte* kernels as she prepared the flat bread for her family's meal. So perhaps tied to a slender thong hung around her throat?

Butterfly Wing grinned and continued striding toward home.

He knew the sounds of the forest and the whispering of water over the streambed's stones. When the tenor of the insect noise or the bird chattering changed, Butterfly Wing would be alerted. Such changes meant a predator was about, and a hunter could suddenly become prey.

Butterfly Wing paused and listened. The sound of moving leaves was different, meaning the breeze came from a new direction. Was a change in weather on the way? The birds were quiet.

He looked to the sky to check the clouds. Something moved in the edge of his glance. Butterfly Wing turned his head, expecting to see some predator. Look as he might, he spotted no threat. But something seemed to skip aside, just ahead of where he looked.

Butterfly Wing stood still and moved only his eyes. Slowly. He noticed an aberration in the air. It was like an impression of some object not truly seen but recognized only after one's glance had moved on to focus on some other thing. Butterfly Wing considered this motionless scrutiny of his surroundings to be purposeful, an action he pursued at his own will. He didn't know he was already spellbound and under the influence of another personality. What his mind told him: He searched for a comprehension of some enigmatic presence that tantalizingly dodged his understanding like a—well, like a butterfly that danced just beyond his reach.

Still moving his eyes slowly, Butterfly Wing managed to keep tracking the aberration as it continued to slide off to the side. It was a wavering of the air—in the vague form of a man—standing upright. It was transparent, for Butterfly Wing could see the trees that stood beyond the shape. The air that formed the object seemed to dance like the invisible smoke above a cook fire.

Such sidewise staring made his eyes itch. Butterfly Wing blinked rapidly.

That's when the thing struck out at him.


*1974 Mexico – Coatzacoalcos and San Lorenzo, Veracruz, Mexico*
"Mexico's been a battleground its entire history. Even its prehistory, after Paleoindians from eastern Asia entered the North American continent and slowly invaded the lower land masses. That's a long war, man."

El Tigre Azul looked across the table at the earnest face of the young man whose long hair shaded the round lenses of his steel-rimmed glasses. He wore faded jeans and a mustard-yellow tee shirt emblazoned with a drawing of large red lips and an extended tongue. Jason Solomon Otterbridge had introduced himself to El Tigre while the luchador stood in tatters alongside his destroyed automobile. The graduate student from the University of California, Berkeley, had accompanied the reporter, Juan Gaceta, to the bombing site. After learning about the Dodge Charger's unfortunate end, Otterbridge had offered to drive El Tigre around in exchange for some information.

"My studies are kind of free form," he'd explained. "I'm looking at the anthropological and sociological ripples of the continual clashes of imperialism across Mexican history," Otterbridge said as he drove El Tigre to his motel so he could wash and change clothes.

The red Volkswagen nearly stalled while it idled at each stop light. That's when Otterbridge would talk faster and start to go breathless before the light changed and he shifted into first gear and coaxed the hump-backed car into motion. After El Tigre cleaned up, the two sat in a small diner and ordered sandwiches and coffee.

The luchador held up a hand to stop the flow of words Otterbridge had released once the men sat down. "You know, Señor Otterbridge, I just had a building blow up around me—"

The student interrupted, "How did that happen, anyway?"

El Tigre held in a sigh. "The police determined *Las Mariposas* tunneled from the shop's basement into the bank's basement and laid a bomb there."

"So that's why you were blown through the door? Instead of buried in the rubble?"

El Tigre shrugged. "I guess."

"Yeah, I see that now." Otterbridge nodded. "I guess that hurt."

El Tigre stared a moment. "*Sí.*"

"Still hurts?"

"*Sí.*"

Otterbridge nodded again. "Yeah. Better being hurt than buried in a bombed building."

El Tigre paused. "*Sí.* So you've been telling me things. And I don't understand any of them. Maybe because, you know, the bomb." He put down his hand and attended to his sandwich.

"Yeah, that makes sense." Otterbridge slurped his coffee. "Let's see, how do I explain this? Okay, yeah." He nodded vigorously. "I'm studying conflict in Mexico, you got that, right? Okay. I learned about you from a guy at Berkeley. He tells me all about the luchador scene, and about seeing you wrestle. And he tells me about how you fight crime like Spider-Man or somebody. And I'm thinking, that's cool. But then—and this is important, yeah? Then he tells me about the crazy other stuff you fight. The monsters. The vampires and werewolves and crazy stuff from Saturday night *Creature Feature*. Yeah?"

El Tigre chewed his sandwich and nodded.

"The problem with so much academic research," Otterbridge continued after another coffee slurp, "is the distance in time from the events described and the lack of specific human focus. But I hear about you, and, hey, I say, here he is! El Tigre Azul, Señor Blue Tiger, he's my specific human focus. Fighting the conflicts that plague Mexico."

El Tigre stared at Otterbridge while he finished his sandwich and chewed his dislike for the notion of being an object of research. "I didn't understand everything you said earlier, but I know you mentioned imperialism. How does fighting—eh, *monstruos* have anything to do with that?"

Otterbridge raised his eyebrows. He crossed his knees and swung one leg, and the toe of his boot tapped one of the table legs. The coffee shivered in their cups. "Yeah, that's a good question. But these monsters, they're also symbols, yeah? Relics of the past that want to conquer the present. Take over and build a new empire of doom. Yeah, that's it! Because vampires and wolfmen, they're all ideas brought over from Europe by the invaders from the old countries. Those aren't homegrown horrors. They are the past empires trying to assert their control over today's Mexico so it will still be the old Mexico, the conquered Mexico, not the modern Mexico making its own way in the world. Yeah, see?"

El Tigre withheld comment. "What do you want?"

"Juan Gaceta, he told me where to find you, and said you're battling these *Las Mariposas*. What's that about?"

El Tigre frowned. "I'm not sure I'm battling them. Mostly I'm being blown up by them." He knitted his fingers together and rested his hands on the table. "I don't know if they are a—a movement or a cult. I'm not even sure what they're trying to do, but they are good at building bombs." He looked at Otterbridge. "I'm not sure that fits in with your— *investigación*."

"Bombs?" Otterbridge's eyes got large in the round lenses when he moved his head. "Oh sure, yeah. Overthrowing authority. That's a conflict with imperialism, sure, absolutely."

El Tigre resisted rolling his eyes. "I've been reading up on this kind of violence since I found out about *Las Mariposas*. It's not just in Mexico." He started ticking off items on his fingers. "The Japanese Red Army attacked the French Embassy in The Hague. I was in France not so long ago. Spanish anarchists kidnapped a Spanish banker in Paris. A store in Saint-Germain-des-Pres was bombed with a grenade. Bombs blew up thirteen buses along the Tour de France. Someone blew up the front of the Cuban Embassy in Paris. Somebody else threw a bomb at the Albanian Embassy there. TransWorld Airlines and Coca-Cola offices were blown up. That's just in Paris! And just in the past few months."

El Tigre's hands waved over the table. "Here in Mexico? Seven bombs exploded in the offices of companies owned in the United States. Someone bombed the Cuban Embassy. The US Vice Consul was kidnapped and murdered. There was an entire wave of bombings at businesses in Mexico City." His fist thumped the table. "*Bombas! Bombas! Bombas!*" He shook his head. "So why do you think my little investigation means anything?"

Otterbridge nodded. "Yeah, see, those anonymous bombs and places with names—people get hurt, sure. But they're missing something. The specific human focus. That's you. See? Yeah, that's you."

El Tigre saw that reasoning with Otterbridge would be a waste of time. "I return to my earlier question: What do you want?"

Otterbridge smiled. "I want to go along with you. Watch what you do."

El Tigre stood up. He was bruised but impatient. "You're the one with a car. Let's go."

After El Tigre checked out of the motel, the two men climbed into Otterbridge's Volkswagen. Before turning the ignition, the student asked, "Where to?"

El Tigre hung his elbow out the window. He wanted to revisit the beach. Instead, he said, "Our mutual friend, Juan Gaceta, told me one of his colleagues heard about *Las Mariposas* operating in San Lorenzo. Got a map?"

"*Si.*" Otterbridge reached behind El Tigre's seat and searched through a nest of papers and booklets.

Nearly three hours later, the luchador could hardly wait for the car to stop so he could escape. The road was rough most of the way, and the Volkswagen had rattled and Otterbridge had nattered continually. El Tigre's attention wandered, but it surfaced occasionally during the trip to catch the student's topic before sinking again into daydreams: "The Mayan wars between cities to control resources and people and to capture victims for sacrifice . . . " and, "The Aztecs were relentless conquerors and they forced more than three hundred city states to pay tribute . . . " and, "The Spanish invasion swept out one empire and replaced it with another, distant rule . . . " and on and on.

San Lorenzo was a small town of only a thousand residents, perhaps fewer. It was surrounded by farms, and the people the Volkswagen passed all looked like members of farming families. Only two or three feet of grass or sandy soil separated the edge of the street from the walls and doorways of the houses and businesses that lined the thoroughfare.

El Tigre waved for his driver to park in a small grassed lot between an auto mechanic's garage and a dressmaker's shop. He wondered how a dressmaker got along in San Lorenzo, for most of the dresses he'd seen appeared homemade of plain materials.

As the two men climbed out of the car, Otterbridge's narrative continued. "The priests and the European armies did their best to destroy everything that displayed pagan influences. Do you know what a codex is? It's a book, made of paper—the Maya made paper, did you know? They used fig tree bark, *amate*."

El Tigre looked up and down the street. He didn't glance at Otterbridge as he asked, "Do you need to take a breath?"

"What? Oh. Yeah, I see. So, there were hundreds of these codices. The Maya recorded their studies of the heavens and events in their history. And of all those, only four still exist. Four! Three are in Europe. Only one remains in this hemisphere. It's amazing."

"Yes, that's amazing." El Tigre had watched the few people on the street disappear by entering doors or the gaps between buildings while he and Otterbridge strolled out of the grass and onto the pavement. "Looks like we have the place to ourselves."

Otterbridge turned his back to El Tigre and gestured farther along the street. "San Lorenzo was an important center for the Olmec culture. If we continue to that end of town, we'll be at the Olmec museum."

"I'm more interested in the present than the past." El Tigre started across the street at a diagonal. "I think that's the place we want."

The frame building's wall facing the street stretched nearly forty feet. Two windows interrupted its expanse, but they had been painted over from the inside. The wall's coating of white paint was far faded, but a black-painted, scrawled B on the single door was new and dark, as yet unweathered by time. El Tigre tried the knob. The door was a sturdy metal one, too substantial for him to kick in, and it was locked. He knocked and waited. No answer.

He directed Otterbridge to stay behind. El Tigre strode around the corner and stepped over empty beer cans and candy wrappers hidden in the tall tangled grass that filled the narrow strip between *Las Mariposas'* building and its neighbor.

The back of the structure offered two doors, one close to the near corner, the other a wide garage door that slid aside on an overhead rail. Both doors were closed.

El Tigre surveyed the area behind the building. A weedy lot stretched to the back of another building—which looked abandoned—that faced the next street over. The luchador turned back to *Las Mariposas'* building. He tried the knob on the nearer door.

It opened.

El Tigre entered.

Most of the interior was dark. Two rectangular columns of brightness shone down from skylights. One was close to the door El Tigre had just entered. Several tables were revealed, each covered with wire, electrician's tape, batteries, wire cutters and other tools. Stacked nearby were bags of fertilizer.

El Tigre thought further investigation would uncover further supplies, but he was already certain that he'd found a bomb-making site.

He'd heard nothing since entering the building, but El Tigre had the sense that someone else was in there with him. He moved deeper into the space. He approached the second lit area under the skylight located beyond the garage door. He stayed out of the direct fall of the light in case whoever else was in there planned to attack once he was clearly visible.

Sleeping bags, blankets and pillows were scattered on the concrete floor. El Tigre found no food containers, no stove, no pots or cooking utensils. Whoever worked here lived elsewhere.

"I am here."

A chill sped up El Tigre's spine when he heard the voice. It came from the darkness filling the far corner at the front of the building.

He advanced toward the source of the voice at a slow pace. As he got farther from the skylight, his vision adapted to the dark better. He could see a form in the corner's murk. Then a row of light bulbs switched on and dazzled the luchador.

He blinked quickly, wary that the figure in the corner might attack while El Tigre was blinded. But the speaker remained in the corner, sitting in a foldable lawn chair with nylon straps. "We are alone here."

As El Tigre's sight returned to normal, he saw the man in the chair was an Indio, of small stature but with well-defined, ropy muscles. He wore a dingy guayabera over faded blue jeans and his feet were naked. "I have seen you," he said. "You have arrived at places where my friends have events. My friends call them *hechos*—acts."

El Tigre narrowed his eyes. "I don't recall seeing you there."

The sitting man shrugged. "I saw you. I have seen you. That you appear at places when these *hechos* occur suggests you have some significance to them. To me."

"I was just there," El Tigre said. He was ready to spring forward or to the side if the sitting man made a threatening gesture, but the Indio appeared completely relaxed. "I only came looking for you in Coatzacoalcos. The other times, I just happened to be there when your *amigos* were up to no good."

The sitting man displayed neither doubt nor agreement. His expression didn't change. "Perhaps so it seemed to you."

"Who are you?"

"That is a question with many answers," the sitting man said. "You may call me Butterfly Wing."

Ah, El Tigre thought, *Las Mariposas.* "What are all these activities by your *amigos*?"

Butterfly Wing tilted his head back so his chin pointed at El Tigre. The luchador couldn't tell if the Indio's eyes remained open. "When I returned to the valley—when I returned to Ciudad de México from El Norte—the air was foul with stinking clouds and ceaseless noise and machines and buildings and an endless swarm of two-legged animals." He brought his face down to look directly at El Tigre. "It was enough."

"Enough? What does that mean?"

Butterfly Wing ignored the question. Instead, he said, "And I have had enough of you."

He flicked his hand.

El Tigre was gone.

## *1500 BC – La Venta*

Butterfly Wing held an arrow before his face. He turned the arrow's point to the left and then to the right, as though he judged the quality of the sharpened edges. But he didn't look at the arrow at all. Instead, he observed Flashing Rain In The Night as he waved to a servant to precede him along the street to the village meeting place.

Flashing Rain In The Night was bedecked in colorful feathers and shells and painted bones as he strode among the houses. Such finery was expected of the village's most honored priest.

In truth, Butterfly Wing didn't watch Flashing Rain In The Night. Instead, Breath Of The Wind followed the priest's movement through Butterfly Wing's eyes. Breath Of The Wind had lived within Butterfly Wing's skin since that day years ago he had encountered the hunter on the trail with the three birds he was taking home. He had lived for a time in Butterfly Wing's home before leaving to join another huddle of people, and he had traveled from place to place over the years, because Butterfly Wing didn't age in the ways of the people with whom he lived. That agelessness was thanks to Breath Of The Wind, who fully enveloped Butterfly Wing's existence, but who kept the hunter's name just the same. It wouldn't help Breath Of The Wind's cause if his lack of aging was noticed. Butterfly Wing had a woman on his mind at the moment he'd lost his brief battle with Breath Of The Wind, a woman named Pink Flower In The Rain. She had attempted to gain Breath Of The Wind's attention when he'd arrived at the village in the guise of Butterfly Wing, but he had rebuffed her. She would be an old, old woman now. Perhaps she was dead.

Breath Of The Wind turned the arrow. He watched Flashing Rain In The Night because the priest was one of those he hated.

Over the years, Breath Of The Wind had observed the rise of the priests. They and the chiefs were in league and imposed habits of living that opposed the old ways, the natural ways that had existed for ages before the two-legged animals arrived. The two-legged animals—the people—had lived like the other animals, moving with the seasons and with the sources of food. But now they settled in one place or another and imposed their will on the plants and the animals. They interfered with the seed-bearing plants so they grew in one place and were harvested.

Breath Of The Wind hated these people's ways. And the sources of these despised behaviors were the people's leaders: the chiefs and the priests.

Butterfly Wing put aside what appeared to be his arrow gazing and stood to follow the path of Flashing Rain In The Night. He remained several yards behind, and he nodded and spoke to people as he passed, for he didn't want the villagers to know he was purposefully tracking the priest. Many of the people recognized Butterfly Wing because he was a fine hunter. Breath Of The Wind had learned how easily a stranger could join a settlement if he could provide welcome services to its members. Breath Of The Wind didn't like the ways of these people, and particularly such wanton killing of the other animals, which pitted the weak people and their tools against stronger and faster animals. Despite the bitterness he tasted when he used these tools so well, he could easily adapt their manners if doing so served his purposes.

Breath Of The Wind knew what Flashing Rain In The Night was about. A meeting of the settlement's people was to occur this night. Both the priest and the chief, Dust In The Flower's Mouth, would lead the meeting. Words would be said and ceremonies performed, all to strengthen the power of these two men over the rest of the settlement. A tension existed between these two leaders, because both held power over the villagers, but each was jealous of the other's influence. Still, both men realized his position depended at least partly on the power of the other, so they were willing to share time with one another in front of their followers—each to strengthen his own role.

However, their trust extended only so far. Thus the chief and the priest met beforehand to make sure all would be as expected during the night's meeting. That was the reason Flashing Rain In The Night's feet carried him to the meeting place during these last daylight hours.

Breath Of The Wind was aware of this tension between the two leaders. Such carefully balanced jealousy was not unusual in each of the settlements in which he'd lived during the past years. This lack of complete trust was a fine thing in Breath Of The Wind's mind, for it suited his purposes very well.

Flashing Rain In The Night reached a broad, low mound surmounted by a stone structure. This was the meeting place. The servant of Dust In The Flower's Mouth already stood at the foot of the mound. For meetings like that planned for the evening, the villagers would gather at the base of the mound, and the chief and the priest would come out of the higher structure and lead the ceremonies required to ensure the people's devotion. For now, only the two servants stood at the bottom of the mound: Flashing Rain In The Face ascended toward the stone hut.

Butterfly Wing passed the mound at an unnoticeable distance. His path half-circled the sacred space, and he carefully made his way through the maze of wattle huts surrounding the base on this side of the mound. These were used as stations for holy work by the acolytes who served the priest in his sacred duties. They were hardly in use presently because no holy days were near, and the evening's ceremony served a secular purpose rather than a sacred one. So Butterfly Wing could easily reach the mound without being seen, for very few people were in the vicinity. In this way he ascended the mound on the side opposite the waiting servants.

A doorway like that entered by Flashing Rain In The Night pierced the stone hut on its opposite side, and Butterfly Wing—crouching so he wouldn't be noticed from the ground—entered by this means.

Moving quietly in the way that earned him recognition as a hunter, sliding effortlessly like a breeze, Butterfly Wing passed through a short, dark tunnel. When he came out into the main room of the structure, the chief and the priest stood conversing in the center of its single chamber, whose floor was carpeted with woven grass mats. Clay figurines stood at the base of the room's walls on all sides.

Dust In The Flower's Mouth had his back to Butterfly Wing. Flashing Rain In The Night saw the hunter enter, his bowstring pulled back, an arrow nocked.

Flashing Rain In The Night's mouth opened as his eyes widened, but before he could speak, two of Butterfly Wing's arrows had flown and lodged in the priest's throat. A third arrow pierced the neck of Dust In The Flower's Mouth. As Flashing Rain In The Night fell to his knees, one more arrow joined the first two sticking out from his throat.

Dust In The Flower's Mouth spun to look at Butterfly Wing. A look of horror stretched his features. The hunter sent two more arrows into the chief's neck.

The two men collapsed on the grass mats. They twitched and bled, but neither had uttered a sound before dying. Butterfly Wing didn't smile. He didn't collect his arrows. He left by the tunnel he'd used to enter the hut. Expressionless, he descended the mound. He went through the maze of wattle huts, and then left the settlement.

Breath Of The Wind made Butterfly Wing's steps fleet. He would find a new village to join.


### *500 BC – La Venta, Mexico*

El Tigre toppled forward in a sudden darkness. He felt no concrete floor beneath his feet. He turned head over heels. His stomach wanted to jet out his ears. His eyes bulged as he entered a vacuum and the pressure within his body pushed outward.

He couldn't breathe.

Then he stopped moving. He was on his hands and knees, a rough texture pressed into his palms, and the wind continued gusting down on his back and past his ears.

The wind stopped.

El Tigre opened his eyes. He was in a room. Not the large room in which he'd found Butterfly Wing. A smaller room. The light was dim. Small lamps burned near three of the four walls, forming a triangle within the room's square. The walls were stone. Woven grass mats covered the floor. Clay figurines were arranged along each wall.

Two dead men lay in the center of the room. They were clothed in some sort of traditional tribal gear. Arrows jutted from their necks. Blood still ran from the wounds, so the killings had occurred very recently.

El Tigre approached the bodies and leaned over them.

A man burst in from a doorway facing El Tigre. He goggled at the sight in the chamber. He screeched a horrible scream, and he chopped the air with a short spear he'd carried at his side.

El Tigre had time only to say, "What is—" before hearing the slap of naked feet approaching from behind the newcomer. Three men tumbled into the room and started gobbling and screaming some language the luchador didn't recognize. He stepped away from the tangled corpses with quick steps. He felt a sharp edge press against the back of his shoulders. A glance showed him another door was open behind him. He ducked—the door was shorter than El Tigre's height—and turned and rushed through the tunnel in which he found himself.

It was growing dark, so he couldn't clearly see when he exited the stone structure. He was running, and when one foot continued downward without touching a flat surface, El Tigre started tumbling down a long, rough slope.

At the bottom, he slammed into the side of a wattle hut. Taking a moment to clear his head, El Tigre heard shouts and screams getting closer. He rolled away from the hut, clambered to his feet, and started running away from the mound. The path here was like a maze. He crashed into the side of a hut and ricocheted from another. The luchador slowed and paid more attention to his progress. He made sure he kept going farther from the mound and was careful to avoid colliding with huts.

He heard rapid footfalls close by. Searchers were also working around the area filled with these huts. El Tigre peeked around corners, then dashed on when no one was in sight.

He had his back to a hut and leaned to the side to peer around the edge. A hole suddenly appeared in the wattle near his head with a chuff that sent bits of dried mud into his face. El Tigre turned. One of the hunters had spotted him. He had something in his hand—despite the failing light, El Tigre recognized it as an *atlatl*, a spear thrower.

El Tigre lunged to the side and rolled to his feet, putting another hut between him and the hunter. He heard the man shout to his fellows. If more showed up carrying spear throwers, they'd soon turn him into a pin cushion.

He finally reached the last hut and charged across a garden plot. On the other side of the cultivated area was a thick forest. El Tigre ran into the trees, putting as much space between him and his pursuers as he could. He knew his outdoor skills were hardly a match for these men who lived in the forest, so he had to think of a way to outwit them.

The shouts were getting closer. El Tigre heard the rattle of leaves and branches as the hunters entered the trees.

He kept pushing forward. His throat began to burn as he panted.

He stopped by a large tree. A hollow gap was visible between the spots where two gnarled roots rose from the soil and joined the trunk. A scorch mark ran from the ground and climbed the tree's trunk up toward the canopy. El Tigre stepped back and looked up. The top of the tree had been blasted away by lightning.

The luchador gripped a branch and started climbing. At the top, he clung to the rough bark and fought to slow his breathing.

El Tigre heard the patter of feet flying past far below. He waited for nearly a minute, then put his face close to the shattered opening at the top of the trunk. A rotted-out hollow was visible at the center of the ragged wood. The luchador counted on it running all through the length of the trunk.

He hooted and moaned long nonsense syllables and gobbling shouts into the hollow's mouth. The cavity amplified the noises and they sounded even weirder emanating from the blasted tree's several openings. After a couple minutes, El Tigre stopped and listened.

His pursuers dressed in feathers and leather and bones. They didn't use guns—they followed the practices of primitive people. El Tigre thought his own mask and urban clothing—a guayabera and chinos—might be exotic enough to make his pursuers think he could be some sort of forest demon, and the noises he'd blown through the tree might frighten them away.

Shivering overwhelmed him suddenly. He bent over the tree's hollow and vomited. He wiped his mouth and clutched the trunk while he trembled.

Adrenaline crash.

How had he gotten here? Where was he? What had that man—Butterfly Wing—done to him? Had he thrown some drug into the air? Was a gas in the room, and was all this chasing through the jungle just a hallucination? Was El Tigre actually rolling on the gritty floor in that bomb-making building?

He shook his head and listened again. If the hooting hadn't had an effect, the reverberating retching should have sent anyone scrambling for cover. The forest was still. Not a sound.

Tired, numb, El Tigre started to clamber back down the branches he'd climbed. The leafy canopy had hidden him from the ground, but it also obscured his view, so as he came through the leaves he peered about. The darkness had deepened and he could make out little on the forest floor.

His foot reached for another branch.

He missed. His weakened grip slipped.

He fell.

As he tumbled, he grabbed for another branch.

It was gone.

*1300 BC – San Lorenzo Olmec Plateau*

Butterfly Wing's eyes were closed. His head was thrown back. His arms were spread slightly from his body. He was like an open flower basking in light. The sun's warmth opened the pores of his skin and made his mind float. The breeze climbed the flanks of the plateau on which Butterfly Wing stood and caressed his eyelashes and carried the scents of the river that split to the northeast and whose forks streamed on either side of this high ground: fish, turtle, snake, frog, fungi clinging to the side of a rotting log that bumped and tumbled along the water's course.

Decay and vitality. Breath Of The Wind preferred these smells over those of the people among whom he dwelt: the sweat, the offal, the scaling puddles of vomit spewed by the drunken revelers after their successful raids into the outlying vassal states.

Breath Of The Wind could hear the air scraping along his nasal passages. After all this time, the many meaty labyrinths of Butterfly Wing's body still felt alien to him, a house whose passages remained a dark maze. The little noises and exhalations of the flora and juices that flowed along their tiny rivers wormed throughout the man's limbs were at times a joy to Breath Of The Wind, but other times they interrupted the intruder's contemplations.

His continual irritation with the world these invading people had built and continued to build rarely had interruption. So he frequently sought isolation to feel the sun and to listen.

Wing feathers combing the air as birds wheeled overhead. The calling caw and responding squawk from the high branches among the trees. The applause of leaves in the gusts of an approaching storm. The whispering sigh of dew evaporating from blades of maize as the sun slowly climbed. The gentle creak of the grass as it bent under the weight of starlight.

Butterfly Wing's eyes opened. His gaze crossed the rooftops of the wattle and daub huts arrayed on the terraces spreading below him along the plateau's sides. Smoke rose in thin ropes from cooking fires and wove a hazy curtain between Butterfly Wing and the trees lining the river.

He turned and surveyed the top of the plateau. Here was the place of the elites. Here were the larger homes and their dwellers daubed with paint and clothed in ornaments and radiant plumes, ostentatious as some mating forest creature. Here were the carvings and the holy sites. This was the place he did his work. This was where he plotted.

Butterfly Wing had put aside his role as hunter many years and villages ago. He realized what the humans valued more than a provider was the miraculous. Someone who could wrangle those massive powers of the earth and sky that had no human-sized handle for managing.

He proclaimed himself a witch.

Proving his worth, building his credibility took no more effort as a witch than as a hunter. And with the maize crops a reliable food source, hunting was held in less regard than the warrior arts. Further, Breath Of The Wind had no desire to send Butterfly Wing into battles with other bands of two-legged animals.

The role of witch allowed him to be strange and unhuman. He could stand a step or two outside the bounds of community expectations for normalcy and still be accepted. He lived on the plateau, but in a far more humble hut than any other dwellings atop the earth's rise. Butterfly Wing's eccentricities were deemed normal behavior for someone who wrestled with the natural world—for how could one tangle with such raw, chaotic powers and come away unscathed? The role also made his seeming agelessness harder to question. And living through several generations of these short-lived two-legged animals made his influence greater among them, both terrace dwellers and those who lived among the elites atop the plateau.

Except for one.

Jaguar Eye had been the high priest for several years. His influence kept the chief's rule in place. His power strengthened the cultural ties that bound the residents together, clarified the rules of living together, and set the expectations for each person who shared the bounties allowed by living on the shoulders of the plateau.

His presence linked daily human life and the power of the gods. He was the interpreter of the savage spirits' wills. The holy carvings couldn't be touched without Jaguar Eye's permission. A new carving couldn't be started until he had judged the stone and anointed it in sacrificial blood.

The chief ruled the plateau and maintained his hand-picked warriors, but the high priest and his lower priests—battle-hardened as well—defined the world by which the plateau existed and kept the gods pleased—or more accurately, sated and at bay. Jaguar Eye's fist kept the dual leadership between him and the chief balanced between the gaze of heaven and that of the underworld. Jaguar Eye was the plateau's paragon of order. In his mind, Butterfly Wing represented anarchy and a threat to the plateau's balance.

Breath Of The Wind recognized that poison in Jaguar Eye's glance, and mirrored it with his own. But not with Butterfly Wing's eyes. The flesh and skin of Butterfly Wing was favored because of his role and he was allowed to reside on the heights of the plateau, despite his strangeness—acceptable because, after all, he was a witch. But within that flesh, Breath Of The Wind hated Jaguar Eye with the same passion the high priest's heart held for the witch.

In this way a war began:

It was Butterfly Wing's habit to wander at night. He would glide among the tree trunks outside the settlement, silent, listening to the sounds of the nocturnal creatures, hearing the padding of night hunters along the ground or gliding through the air. He inhaled the river breezes.

One evening when most of the plateau and terraces' people slept and only the stars lit his path, he had paused to listen to the breathing of an owl high in a tree sixty long steps from where he stood. The owl—a mighty predator—was inhaling when an unexpected hitch interrupted its breath.

Butterfly Wing had already detected the cause of this interruption. He had heard a delicate step in the decaying matter between the roots of a tree and the disturbance of the air that followed. The witch stepped aside from the position he'd been holding. A rush of the forest's breath passed by his arm and a heavy thump sounded from the tree trunk by which he'd been standing. A spear's head was buried in the trunk, and its shaft vibrated with the energy it released.

The witch didn't chase his attacker. Breath Of The Wind had recognized the man's smell and his tread as he'd slipped away after realizing his attack had failed. It had been a warrior—not one of Jaguar Eye's priests nor one of the chief's guards, but one of those raiders who the witch knew was devoted to the high priest's words.

Allowing his attacker time to escape, Butterfly Wing's thews swelled to pull the spear from where it had lodged in the trunk. The head had been driven deeply into the wood, so the witch knew it had been flung with an *atlatl*, which could speed a spear with many times more power than one thrown without its help. Once Butterfly Wing pulled the spear free, he made his way back to his hut, making sure he was unseen. Once home, he hid the spear.

Many months later, when a raiding party from the plateau had battled a band of opposing warriors and was returning home with prisoners, the victors were surprised to find the body of one of their number. None of them had seen him fall during the attack. What was most remarkable: he was skewered by one of his own spears.

A few weeks after Butterfly Wing avoided a thrown spear in the dark, he was walking around one of the massive carved heads that rested atop the plateau. As his feet rustled the mixture of red sand and yellow gravel that covered the paths where the elites lived, he made sure his steps drew no closer than a yard away from the large stone as he circled it. He paused to gaze at its face. Its unblinking eyes appeared to stare in return, inscrutable as his own. It would've been impossible for an observer to determine whether Butterfly Wing studied the head or was simply staring blindly while lost in thought.

The witch was drawn from his reverie by one of the couriers who moved messages between the terraces and the plateau. A woman in one of the wattle huts was experiencing a difficult pregnancy, and Butterfly Wing's help was requested.

The people here were both sturdy and hearty, even in their birthing, but such appeals weren't unusual. Breath Of The Wind's feelings about the two-legged animals were sometimes indecipherable even to the witch, but after continuing to stare at the colossal stone head for several beats longer, Butterfly Wing made a gesture. The courier turned and walked away, and the witch followed.

In the hut to which the courier had led him, Butterfly Wing's open hand was spread on the pregnant woman's belly. He didn't look at her, but took in the carved figurines arranged in the living space. These small effigies had meaning for Jaguar Eye's world, and their presence here meant this family was held within the palms of the high priest's influence. Breath Of The Wind considered that as he recalled the spear that had been flung at him.

The woman's belly trembled against his hand. Her anxiety at the witch's presence—even though she'd called for him—made her breathing ragged. Breath Of The Wind's fingers reached invisibly through her flesh to the sprout within her womb. The child she carried was soured and would not live. Butterfly Wing turned his stare to her face and her eyes widened. His lips parted to tell her what he'd learned. He paused.

He thought again of Jaguar Eye's creature, who had attempted to kill him.

"The child will live," Butterfly Wing said to the woman. "When it is born, bring it to me."

He turned and strode from the hut to return to the plateau. The woman hadn't said a word. The witch's presence had made her unable to speak.

Months after the warrior who'd attacked Butterfly Wing had died during a skirmish, a courier came again for Butterfly Wing. The woman had given birth and now awaited him. The witch followed the messenger. The woman stood on the terrace nearest the plateau's top level. She held a baby boy, his face twisted and red as he mewled with hunger.

Butterfly Wing stared at the infant dispassionately as he would gaze at any inanimate object his path would come across. He glanced at the mother, whose lips trembled. While she held the baby, Butterfly Wing put his hands around the child's head. Tufts of black hair stood between his spread fingers. The witch said nothing, just glared into the boy's red face. Then he lowered his hands.

Butterfly Wing's glare moved to the woman. "Care for him well. Raise him to be strong. I will see him again."

Without another word, the witch turned and ascended to the plateau's top once more.

Afterward the mother, River Flashing Light, while grateful to the witch for helping with the birth and health of the child who had been named Sun Rising Mist, remained skittish as a deer and glanced frequently to the left and right, always expecting to see Butterfly Wing approaching.

Despite Butterfly Wing's declaration to the woman, he didn't turn his attention to Sun Rising Mist for several years.

In that time, Breath Of The Wind brooded atop the plateau or during walks through the thick forest. The witch dealt with the issues of the living as they called on his particular skills. One of the gardeners complained about a toothache. Butterfly Wing stuck fingers into the man's mouth and poked a molar. Over the next few days the pain would drain from the tooth and migrate to his elbows and knees.

One of the artists ruined two fingers while carving a stela to be set along the approach to the high priest's blood altar. The pain was great and ringing through the man's head and body. He staggered and couldn't speak, could only groan and gesture vaguely. Butterfly Wing looked at the hand, then glanced at the eyes of the two men who'd brought the artist to him. The witch spoke to the artist: "Your hand is angry at your carelessness. It wants to kill you. It will kill you." He directed the men to chop off the artist's hand at the wrist and cauterize the stump with a stone heated in a fire.

A woman saw spots floating across her eyes. Butterfly Wing spat in her eyes. The spots would fade, but soon her ears would echo with the cawing of birds that wouldn't cease throughout the daylight hours or during the nights as she tried to sleep.

Feigning disinterest, Jaguar Eye saw these interactions between the witch and the people. He watched the ones who lived in the wattle huts approach Butterfly Wing and ask for succor from their ills no matter how often his ministrations resulted in a different or often worse pain. Butterfly Wing's relations with the people happened on a small, intimate scale, while the high priest's activities enveloped the entire community in a cultural embrace. Jaguar Eye performed on a higher plane than the witch. But the priest was jealous of Butterfly Wing's many small, human-scaled performances. Jaguar Eye believed the witch's encounters undermined the priest's power.

During the intervening years, three more children had expanded River Flashing Light's brood. Two boys had joined Sun Rising Mist and their father in tending the maize and sunflower crops. The youngest, a daughter, worked with a busy corps of girls and women using dyes and feathers and shells plucked from the rivers and bits of glittering stones to assemble finery for the priests and elites who lived atop the plateau. The four children did their work well, but the oldest—Sun Rising Mist—had a brooding, recalcitrant manner that made him nearly silent among the other family members.

The day Butterfly Wing's silhouette had first appeared framed by the darkness of the hut's door, with the glaring sunlight behind him, both dread and hope swelled in River Flashing Light's chest alongside the baby in her belly. The morning of the witch's second appearance, when he again was a dark effigy backlit in the hut's door, only dread thumped behind her breast bone. Butterfly Wing offered no word of greeting: that was not his way. Instead, he asked, "Where is he?"

Who the witch meant was no mystery to River Flashing Light. The woman answered, "He is with the men. In the crops."

Butterfly Wing turned and left without a further word.

Beyond the foot of the plateau were scattered a number of *islotes* on which crops were grown. These agricultural islets had been built up over generations by workers digging borrow pits and dredging river mud and hauling and dumping it so crops would escape being swamped in the floodplain. These efforts secured the harvest and ensured the reliability of the plateau community's food supply, which included maize, squash, sweet potatoes, beans, sunflowers, and papaya. Without asking further questions from anyone, Butterfly Wing descended the plateau's terraces and approached a particular *islote*. He climbed its shoulder until he reached the top.

Custom said anyone approaching the workers in the crops spoke to the headman first. Butterfly Wing didn't seek the headman but simply trudged into the maize field. He could feel the boy's presence among the stalks. He walked right to him, where Sun Rising Mist carried a staff and made sure the irrigation trench was clear and flowing as it should. When Butterfly Wing stood beside the boy, the twelve-year-old stopped his work and looked the witch in the face. After a pause, he dropped his tool and started for the headman, who glared at Butterfly Wing.

Stopping before the headman, Sun Rising Mist spoke. "I am leaving. I will be working with the priests." Waiting for no response, the boy turned and walked away.

The headman finally shook his words loose from his surprise. "Have you talked to the priests? Do they know?"

He received no answer. He saw only Sun Rising Mist's back as the boy walked away. The headman turned and saw Butterfly Wing leaving as well. The witch didn't accompany Sun Rising Mist but walked a different direction.

Butterfly Wing didn't know how the encounter between Sun Rising Mist and the priests had gone. But that night a courier arrived at his door and summoned him to the terrace nearest the plateau's top level, where years before he'd met River Flashing Light as she held her newborn. This time Sun Rising Mist's father, Vine Winding Branch, awaited the witch. The man expected no greeting from Butterfly Wing, so when the witch stood before him Vine Winding Branch demanded, "Where is my son?"

Respect and fear pulled at the man's mind, but when he finally spoke, anger swept those feelings aside and fired the father's words.

Butterfly Wing answered without passion, "He is not with me."

"Sun Rising Mist is with the priests!"

"Then that is where he is."

Whatever fear about the witch's power Vine Winding Branch had carried had now evaporated. He shook his fist. "This is your doing!"

Butterfly Wing still showed no emotion. "If Sun Rising Mist went to the priests, that is his doing."

Furious exasperation animated Vine Winding Branch's face and body. "He went because you told him to do so!"

"I said nothing to him. If he went to the priests, and they kept him, that is between Sun Rising Mist and the priests. I have nothing to do with the priests and their work. Go to them." Butterfly Wing turned and strode away.

"I went to them!" Vine Winding Branch shouted. "They would not speak to me!"

Butterfly Wing continued to his home. Whatever barriers Vine Winding Branch broke to display such anger to the witch still wouldn't allow him to follow Butterfly Wing onto the plateau's top level. Such a place was not for him. His fists clenched and tears running from his eyes to his chin, Vine Winding Branch watched Butterfly Wing until the witch disappeared, then the man's shoulders slumped. He returned home to Sun Rising Mist's weeping mother.

Anyone who didn't hear the exchange between Vine Winding Branch and Butterfly Wing heard of it by the following dawn. Because eccentric behavior was expected from the witch, no one was truly surprised.

What Jaguar Eye and the other priests made of this, they didn't say and no one was expecting to hear any pronouncements related to this brief bubble of rumor unless it affected the wellbeing of the community as a whole. The caste of priests remained aloof from gossip.

Years passed.

Butterfly Wing tended the ailments and appeals he received. He continued his occasional wanderings, sometimes during the day and sometimes at night. He would detect the cautious hunters who stalked him. Always he evaded them and their diligent efforts to kill him, and never did he let on he was aware of their pursuit and their murderous missions.

Vine Winding Branch and River Flashing Light grew older and died. Their children continued their work—two sons in the crops, the daughter with the elites' finery until her skills allowed her to tutor those younger than her, and Sun Rising Mist among the priests. As he grew in maturity, he ascended in the hierarchy of the priesthood until he bowed only to Jaguar Eye's authority. The high priest had aged as well, and wrinkles furrowed his face in a design more complex than any irrigation map. While in his role he had outlived three chiefs.

Butterfly Wing appeared no older than when he had first appeared at the plateau.

During those years a unique building was erected on the plateau's top. Built on a raised platform, like all the structures on the plateau's heights, red sand plastered its mud walls and red gravel covered its floors. Basalt, typically hauled great distances from its source for the plateau's artists to carve into colossal heads depicting rulers and gods, was used in this new palace for stair treads and as columns for roof supports. This ornate building, when complete, was the new home for the plateau's chief. An adjoining structure—less glorious in its details but still ornately decorated—was provided for use by the community's most highly skilled artists.

In this elite workshop were carved the giant heads that marked the ritual path laid out north-to-south across the heights of the plateau, along which the chief and the priests paraded for the highest ceremonies. Also produced were stelae and memorial thrones that marked significant sites atop the plateau and throughout the community.

This workshop also was the repository of older carved stones that were to be used for some new purpose. Butterfly Wing had seen carried into the studio a colossal head representing the chief who'd ruled the plateau when the witch had first arrived—he had died generations ago, and no one was alive who remembered his reign. Months later the stone head left the workshop in several parts: as a new ceremonial throne and as several *manos* and *metates* used for grinding maize and seeds. Unrevealed on Butterfly Wing's face, Breath Of The Wind smiled: what would the blood sacrifice used to dedicate the original giant carving have thought of this new use for old stone?

One night, while wandering through the forests and deftly eluding any of Jaguar Eye's stalkers, Butterfly Wing went hunting.

His hunt had begun several days earlier, when he'd had one of the rubber makers fashion three items for him. The man had mixed the juice from a twining vine with latex brought in by the rubber tree harvesters, then he had worked the mixture until he'd made what the witch had ordered: three rubber bags, two with a hollow ear on one side. Each bag was roughly the size of an open hand.

Butterfly Wing had pierced the plain bag several times around the top edge of its opening, and he'd threaded a cord through the holes, allowing him to close and secure the open bag.

He took the three items with him during his hunt.

After midnight, Butterfly Wing stopped at the edge of a clearing. He stood by a tree trunk and listened. He shut out the arboreal sounds and focused on the grasses and vines before him: the tiny footsteps of a mouse, the sliding hiss of a snake's belly scales along the ground, the cautious tapping of peccary hooves crossing the glade, the rustle—

The rustle of a marine toad through grass blades that arched over its humped back—this sound was distinct from the other life noises in the clearing.

This toad was Butterfly Wing's quarry.

The witch removed the two eared bags from where a rope wound about his waist held them. He pulled one over each hand, using them as rubber mittens. His thumbs went into the hollow ears.

Quieter than the mouse, Butterfly Wing advanced. Stealthier than the snake, he struck: He caught up the toad in his two gloved hands. While Butterfly Wing held the squirming creature against the ground with one hand—without its legs extended, the toad was about the size of a fist—the witch plucked the third bag from his rope belt, held open its mouth with his free hand, and dropped his prize inside. He quickly drew shut the cord and knotted it.

Butterfly Wing returned to the trees, where he swung the bag sharply against a tree trunk. The toad stopped its struggles. The witch stood quietly and listened for several minutes. Satisfied, he strode homeward.

He hung the little corpse from a rafter and allowed it to dry. Butterfly Wing was careful in handling the toad, because its skin was highly poisonous, and a single touch could prove deadly. Once the toad had thinned and wrinkled like a tomatillo husk, the witch took it down and crushed it with a small *mano* and *metate*, setting aside the bones. He poured the resulting powder inside a shallow jar carved from a stone and placed its lid snugly on top before tying a red-dyed cord around it so the top wouldn't slide off.

Two evenings later, Butterfly Wing joined the priests and artists and other elites during their peregrinations along the pebbled paths traced among the colossal heads, ceremonial thrones, and other sacred carvings arranged by holy decree across the plateau heights. The sounds of gravel and sand disturbed by slowly stepping feet was interrupted only by occasional low chanting from one or another priest whose course reached a particular monument requiring sung obeisance. This sacred parade was lit only by the stars and the crescent of the waning moon.

To Breath Of The Wind, this barest hint of light was bright as daytime.

The darkness allowed Butterfly Wing to pass close by Sun Rising Mist as the priest walked in the opposing direction. In that half second of proximity, the witch spoke no word but handed off the cord-wrapped jar loaded with toad powder to Sun Rising Mist. The jar disappeared under his cloak, and the priest didn't pause in his stride, made no sign, revealed no expression, demonstrated no recognition for the witch.

Butterfly Wing and Sun Rising Mist were no closer than twenty yards through the rest of the night.

The procession continued uninterrupted in the dark until the palest suggestion of dawn first became visible in the east.

The night of the new moon was quiet on the plateau. The following midday, before the assembled population, Jaguar's Eye would perform a ritual sacrifice on a basalt altar. During the black hours before sunrise, in a temple far more modest than the chief's Red Palace, Sun Rising Mist assisted the high priest in his ablutions as he prepared for his ceremonial duties.

Butterfly Wing had glided past the pair of priestly guards standing at the temple's entrance. Breath Of The Wind's abilities allowed him to move silently and unseen to the high priest's most private rooms. Hidden in the deeper darkness of a corner, not even breathing, the witch watched Sun Rising Mist remove Jaguar's Eye robe and other raiment, leaving the elderly high priest clothed only in the necklace and bangles of his office.

Sun Rising Mist bathed the old man slowly, carefully. He poured oils in a small bowl, mixed them with herbs, then brushed them across the high priest's limbs with a long feather.

All the while Jaguar's Eye chanted in a low, murmuring voice.

From a low altar, Sun Rising Mist lifted a shallow jar Butterfly Wing recognized as the one he'd given the young man.

Sun Rising Mist kneeled before Jaguar's Eye, lifted the jar, and tossed its contents onto the face, neck, and chest of the old man.

Jaguar's Eye gasped. His eyes gaped at Sun Rising Mist. He shivered and gritted his teeth. His skin blistered and peeled back from his flesh. He raised his arms.

Sun Rising Mist took one step back.

Jaguar's Eye began to vibrate, and his eyes flashed green. Light swam across his face like branches of lightning in the night sky. Then his face changed.

His face was that of a jaguar.

One of his arms whipped across his body and his clawed hand ripped open Sun Rising Mist's throat.

Standing in an spreading blood puddle over the dying Sun Rising Mist, the priest's old body continued to vibrate. No longer did it appear old and flaccid: now its frame carried a young man's mighty thews and the pale spots of a jungle cat. Jaguar's Eye had yet to voice a single howl or hiss despite his struggle against the toad's poison.

While the priest continued to flail, Butterfly Wing silently fled through the dark.

As he descended the terraces below the heights of the plateau and passed among the thick-boled trees in the forest beyond the crop *islotes*, the only sound Butterfly Wing made was that of his panting.

*1300 BC – San Lorenzo Olmec Plateau*

El Tigre Azul opened his eyes.

He was no longer falling. The sun shone directly overhead. He stood at the edge of a forest and faced a clearing. Crossing the open space was a group of fiercely painted warriors, nearly naked and marked with blood, leading a line of men linked by ropes tied around their necks. The prisoners were also painted like warriors, also marked with blood, and their hands were bound. All were Indios.

El Tigre saw this in two blinks. He also saw a lone warrior charging toward him and swinging a heavy club. The attacker was ululating a fierce howl.

As the club came down toward his head, El Tigre dodged under the swing and drove his shoulder into the warrior's belly. The two men tumbled. They rolled together and then apart, and the warrior returned to his feet in less than a heart beat. He swung the club again.

El Tigre feinted, pivoted, and slammed his elbow into the back of the Indio's neck. The club went flying. He grabbed the warrior, spun him about, and clapped his hands on the sides of the man's head. Stunned, the warrior couldn't resist as El Tigre whipped him around once more and threw him to the ground.

El Tigre leapt atop his attacker, pinned the man's arms to the earth with his knees, and ground the warrior's face into the dirt. Angry, con-fused, and fed up, the luchador hissed at the man's ear, "I am a warrior, too."

He noticed then the other warriors shouting. El Tigre looked up. The prisoners stared at him, goggle-eyed. Several victors of whatever raid-ing party he'd stumbled onto rushed forward, halfway between their line of captives and where El Tigre fought, and made humble gestures while laying their weapons on the grass—clubs, maces, stone axes—before backing away.

Puzzled, El Tigre watched this display several moments before he realized what he was seeing. *They think I'm a god.*

He stood up, then lifted his fallen attacker and tossed him at the pile of weapons. He shouted at the group—something incomprehensible even to his own ears—and waved his arms in a threatening manner. Still a little dazed, he thought he may have growled.

Two of the raiders collected their fallen comrade, then the entire group trotted around El Tigre and into the forest behind him. Those who were still armed prodded the prisoners. When the last of the warriors fled into the forest, El Tigre waited a beat, and then followed them. He needed to know where he was, and this group of guards and prisoners looked to be headed somewhere specific.

Once again El Tigre had arrived somewhere without any evidence of how it had happened. His head spun, not just from the attack, but also the—recent?—flight from the spear throwers that had led to his climbing the lightning-shattered tree. Further, he remained bewildered by the complete mystery about what was happening to him and how.

Was he still rolling on the floor at Butterfly Wing's feet, bound in some hallucination tightly as with chains?

He shook his head and trudged on, listening to the warriors' advance ahead of him, careful not to lose their trail. Intent on these sounds, El Tigre didn't notice three shadows peel away from tree boles and begin to follow him. They drew closer, silent as breezes. He had no notion what was going to happen before a cloud blew into his path from behind him. He'd already inhaled the dust as he spun to face a possible new threat, and he was already falling into unconsciousness as his legs gave way.

When El Tigre's eyes opened again, his hands and ankles had been bound, and he was suspended by lashings at his wrists and knees from a long staff carried at each end by an Indio. His mind wheeled for several minutes as the rhythm of their march lulled him sleepward again. Finally, the last effects of the drug dust having fallen away, El Tigre wondered that the warriors had returned to subdue him after demonstrating obeisance to him in the clearing.

After twisting his neck a bit and getting a better look at his captors, he realized they weren't the same soldiers he'd encountered earlier. These wore sashes of brilliant scarlet, and the designs painted on their faces differed from those of the other men.

The face designs puzzled him. They looked familiar. He pondered this as he was carried through the thick forest. The men remained silent as they trudged along. At one point they stopped, lowered him to the ground, and the carrier in the rear took over from the man in the lead position. A third man, who'd been walking parallel to the carriers, picked up the rear of the staff. El Tigre's staff was hefted onto their shoulders, and the march continued.

That's when El Tigre recalled where he'd seen the face designs. He'd seen carved Olmec artifacts at various museum exhibitions during the years—colossal heads, jade axe heads, ceremonial statues and more—and jaguar heads or were-jaguars were features common to many of these. The details were very distinctive and memorable. And the paint on these men's faces resembled those lines.

These men weren't warriors like the group El Tigre had encountered in the clearing. His captors were monks, or priests, or worshippers of an ancient jaguar god.

He hadn't heard of any jaguar cults springing up. But with so many people organizing into groups who had a bone to pick with current society, he'd probably missed a few. Maybe this jaguar crew hadn't yet made the newspapers by setting off bombs in public places.

Bombs. Just like the men who'd chased him with *atlatls*, this gang didn't rely on guns.

El Tigre squeezed his eyes tightly shut. *Where can I possibly be? How did I get here?*

The puzzle distracted him from the pains in his limbs. For a few moments.

After dark, they arrived at a large settlement. The many torches posted around the area provided enough light for El Tigre to make out some details despite the disadvantage of his position. They passed cultivated fields raised several feet above the level of the main grounds. Many residences lay beyond those gardens, and the place appeared to have a thriving population.

When they arrived at the foot of a tall hillock, one of the priests spoke to a man who appeared to be waiting there. This person ran up the hill. While his captors stood in place, El Tigre craned his neck to see more, and saw that what he thought was a hill actually extended to the left and right and formed a tall plateau. When the man returned—El Tigre decided he was some sort of messenger—the priests started carrying him up the hillside.

More homes stood on the slopes in terraced areas. The amount of work required to build and maintain this community—El Tigre was amazed he'd never heard of this place. He remained baffled about his location, and he couldn't comprehend the language he'd heard spoken.

The priests stopped just below the top of the plateau. They placed El Tigre on the ground, removed the staff, and prodded him to his feet. The luchador could hardly stand upright.

A backlit figure stood at the lip of the plateau and stared down at El Tigre. Someone brought forward a torch. The light revealed an angry-faced man wearing a robe of scarlet feathers. The light also revealed the luchador. Seeing the captive and his distinctive mask, whose stripes represented his identity as The Blue Tiger, the robed man's eyes widened and his face matched the color of the feathers wrapping him. His mouth opened to a fierce shriek. The priests quailed. The screaming man threw forward his open right hand.

An invisible fist slammed into El Tigre's chest. He was flung backwards off the slope. He spun in the air and the torchlight wheeled in his eyes.

El Tigre kept flying backward and down. When he tensed his body to strike the ground of the hillside, he continued tumbling through the air. He didn't touch down. He just whirled and fell, the wind whipped past, and he fell, and the lights disappeared.

*400 AD – Land of the Maya: Teotihuacan and Cholula*

Butterfly Wing became a nomad with no tribe, a wanderer through the forests and swamps and grasslands. He walked to the eastern coast and looked at the ever-moving sea. He watched the sun climb and disappear and saw the moon send quicksilver dancers onto the waves.

The communities he had lived among spread and dwindled and disappeared in the way of gathered people. The two-legged animals hacked at the vines and trees and gave birth and died and joined other clans. New villages rose on the ruins of the old and eventually hid the earlier signs of habitation. The generations rose and passed and the old men and women told the children of legends of a whispering ghost that hunted men among the giants of the forest.

Breath Of The Wind cut them down when they were alone or in groups trudging along the game trails through the undergrowth. The stories that passed among the men sometimes gave him names, sometimes not. They told of an angry ghost gliding below the leafy canopies where shadow and light danced in ways to confuse the senses.

In all cases he was known as a terrifying predator.

Butterfly Wing visited the plateau where he had feuded so surreptitiously with Jaguar's Eye. The *islotes* were tangled with weeds, the terraces and the heights were abandoned. The Red Palace was empty and falling to ruin. The red-and-yellow sand-and-gravel paths among the monuments were overgrown, and erosion had made the colossal heads tumble.

He drifted further inland to the Valley of Mexico where once Breath Of The Wind had swum through the tall grasses before the two-legged animals appeared from the north. Butterfly Wing sought no public role during the years he lingered in the vicinity. During that time, a great city was built by a vigorous and sanguine people who raised monumental structures for worship and blood-letting. They built a tremendous road that connected scores of pyramidal temples where they displayed their barbaric splendor. Butterfly Wing watched. Breath Of The Wind saw the people raise and expand their city and he thought of ants. Furious, deadly ants.

Eventually thousands lived and worked there. Butterfly Wing chafed at their thronging presence. Cutting out members of this herd without notice was a simple matter for him thanks to his non-human power. He whittled hundreds of lives from the city's population. No one in authority noticed. Or cared.

But the tenor of the culture changed as more immigrants arrived and swelled the ranks of an already massive number of people centered on this place. The forests were cut down and the hillsides dug to make lime and to snatch stones from the earth to build the city and its wonders. The rains, once so common and nourishing, fled the valley. The poorer workers bore the burdens resulting from the elite classes' demands for grandeur. Breath Of The Wind detected disturbances in the land and in the inhabitants' words and expressions like distant thunder in a growing and slowly approaching storm.

Butterfly Wing wandered again, away from the mighty city in the highlands, because he knew the inhabitants would destroy themselves in a far more dramatic way than he would manage to attempt.

He climbed out of the crowded basin and trekked eastward bearing south across the mountains. He descended to the plains. Far to the south rose two volcanic peaks breathing clouds into the sky. Butterfly Wing paused and drew clean air into his lungs and into his ears the sounds of the world around him that included nothing uttered or caused by a human being: the rattling whir of grasshoppers wheeling through the air; the whisper of moths' wings; the twirtling songs of birds.

He paused for several years.

He couldn't escape the people, however. At the edge of Butterfly Wing's sight a community arose and expanded into the plains. After generations, they erected a grand pyramidal structure. It differed from those he'd seen in the Valley of Mexico, but its height created a dramatic feature on the flatlands.

One day Butterfly Wing walked into the city to look at this manmade hillock. He ignored the crowds stirring in the marketplaces and plazas just as they ignored him. He directed his steps to the pyramid.

Many yards from its base he stopped and examined its details. It was a stepped pyramid. Each inwardly sloped level was interrupted by another whose sides were perpendicular to the ground and topped by a flat surface, like a table. Decorative panels were painted with intricate insect designs.

Butterfly Wing wandered around the city for several hours. He observed the inhabitants and studied their buildings and the objects created by the artisans. As dusk approached, he walked away and meandered into the plains toward the distant volcanoes. The people's busyness exhausted his patience. He knew they would crow proudly to the sun and then would collapse, as all the others of their kind had done.

Perhaps he would have to do nothing. Perhaps they would eventually destroy themselves and their bones would be covered by windblown soil—or, perhaps, volcanic ash—and Breath Of The Wind could again live peacefully in a world without the two-legged animals.

There were just so many of them. Like ants.


*1380 AD – Land of the Aztec: Tenochtitlan*
A clawlike hand on El Tigre's biceps jerked the luchador forward. The battler stumbled along. A discordant roaring pulsed in his ears. Long, curling sea waves rolled from somewhere behind his head, through his skull, and crashed against the front of his brain.

He shook his head and a whirring gyroscope toppled off its perch and rolled and bounced inside his rib cage like a pin ball in an arcade machine.

El Tigre's eyelids dragged open.

He stood in a line with other men, about a dozen, each escorted by another man. The escorts were dressed in some sort of barbaric ceremonial finery. The rest of the men were naked. El Tigre looked down. He still wore his guayabera and chinos, but they were tattered and unrepairable.

The sun blazed on his head and his mask chafed. He and the others stood on a stone platform raised over a clamoring crowd—the source of the roaring he'd heard. The platform was one of several pyramidal structures rising above a huge paved plaza.

He looked ahead to see where his escort was leading him. EL Tigre's sight was jittering about. He finally focused on the head of the line. A man painted brilliant scarlet awaited the naked men. He stood over a large blunt stone, also painted red. Beside that large rock stood a carved figure, reclining horizontally.

El Tigre's eyes snapped into focus. The red man wasn't painted. Blood covered his face and torso. Blood streamed down his raised arms and dripped from his elbows. The blunt stone was an altar. The reclining figure was a *chacmool* holding a platter. The platter was heaped with hearts, ripped from the men who had preceded those now in line.

What El Tigre uttered was incomprehensible to his own ears. He turned and snatched up his escort—some sort of under-priest, he guessed—and lifted the smaller man overhead. He tossed him over the platform's edge. The figure bounced and tumbled down the stepped incline and the mob's shouts turned to screams.

El Tigre descended rapidly behind the man he'd thrown. When his human projectile struck the people at the foot of the platform, those in front tumbled backwards and knocked down those around them. El Tigre followed the chaos, barreling through and bowling over others thrown off balance by the hurtling priest and those he struck. He charged forward, swinging and kicking as he went, and burst through the outer edge of the gathering.

From the height of the platform, he'd spotted the edge of the city. He galloped fast as he'd ever run.

His quick glances told him the city nearly matched depictions of Tenochtitlan's glory he'd seen during museum tours. How could he be in a life-size recreation of a city that had fallen to conquest and ruin centuries ago?

The luchador's mind worked over this puzzle while he rushed out of the plaza and into an open market, creating confusion and narrowly avoiding calamity more than once. He eventually found his way into a residential area and sought narrower and darker and less appealing lanes and alleys. Twisting and dodging and backtracking and looping around, he finally came to a sprawling cluster of hovels that lay on the edge of the urban area. Deep inside this precinct, he found a suitable patchwork hut that looked abandoned—or in such a sorry state that it should be so—and hid within.

El Tigre crouched in a dark corner and watched disturbed dust rise and fall in crooked slants of light. His chest heaved as he fought for breath. He covered his mouth with a forearm to block the noise of his gasping. The clamor from the searchers swelled and diminished. He could hear the continuing murmur of their search through the neighborhood for several hours.

By dark, he remained undiscovered. While he'd waited, he finally accepted the realization that the normal-looking Butterfly Wing had somehow thrown him back into time. Or made him think so, at least. But El Tigre admitted that all his experiences had seemed very realistic to have actually been hallucinations. And he'd had enough encounters with the strange and unexplainable to shake his head and think, *Why is this so hard to believe?*

Finally settling on the notion that he'd been pitched into the past, El Tigre had no intention of being stuck there. But how could he escape?

After some long considerations, he decided to go to San Lorenzo. After all, that was where he'd encountered Butterfly Wing. El Tigre would have to leave Tenochtitlan and cross the mountains and then head southeast toward the coast.

Three hours after dark, El Tigre left his hideaway. Slow, wary of patrols or anyone else who might spot him, he moved through the neighborhood toward the city's edge. Finally leaving the last structure behind, El Tigre began trotting toward the foothills, maintaining a steady pace to move quickly but without tiring out. He remained careful to watch so he wouldn't encounter anyone along the way. He just had to reach the mountains.

After that, he only had to travel three hundred kilometers.

### *1380 AD – Land of the Aztec: Tenochtitlan*

Butterfly Wing walked north out of the wavering haze of the plains and trekked into the mountains and down into the Valley of Mexico once again. It had been his home so long ago before the two-legged animals arrived and he felt drawn back to this place. He had wandered and watched the humans for so long, fascinated and repulsed by their strange ways, their little wars and rituals.

A new city covered the ruins of the city he'd left generations ago. A powerful city-state to which other localities paid obeisance, it was a community of bright plazas and mighty constructions that lifted the two-legged animals close to the sun, which served as audience to their bloody performances. Great stages and lesser stages, each with its own crowds, each with its own performers displayed in pomp and audacity.

Butterfly Wing drifted through the markets and the alleys and the broad avenues and observed and listened. Despite his disdain, some of what he heard intrigued Breath Of The Wind.

As in other places he'd been, the priests held great power here. And their influence was divided among several factions. Precariously balanced rivalries could tip into violence thanks to the slightest flutter of an eyelash or an inadvertent smile. Butterfly Wing heard mentioned several times the name of a particular priest: The Jaguar. His popularity had been increasing during recent months, and this singular attention had made him the focus of hostility from others in the priestly role.

Butterfly Wing listened and determined where he might see this Jaguar. He made sure he was in the crowd at the next ceremony at which El Jaguar would preside.

He had learned that this city participated in small wars with neighboring city states. From the regular clashes between rival warriors, prisoners were brought in to serve as sacrifices in the public ceremonies. Butterfly Wing attended the next such event. Standing as a member of the tightly packed mob, choking on the fumes of human sweat and foul breath, he watched as lower-level priests escorted a line of drugged prisoners and placed them, one at a time, on the slaughter stone set on a raised terrace within sight of the crowd.

This sacred structure was hardly the largest of those standing in the city. But from the ceremonies Butterfly Wing had witnessed since entering the environs, the number of observers here was far greater than any he'd seen at the other events, even those at much larger pyramidal altars. Clearly the words he'd overheard were true, and the priest leading the activities at this site had more followers than many of his peers despite performing at this lesser temple.

Beside the altar stood a blood-spattered *chacmool*, a reclining figure of carved stone on whose belly rested a golden bowl holding the steaming hearts of the sacrifices. By the slaughter stone posed the priest Butterfly Wing came to see. His arms were raised to the sky as he invoked the sun or some other sky god's attention while the remains of one victim were pulled away and tossed to the crowd and the next sacrifice was led into position.

Butterfly Wing pressed through the bodies surrounding him until he stood at the front of the crowd and his view of The Jaguar was clear.

Red dripped from the priest's arms up to his elbows. Scarlet spattered and spotted his face and chest. Plumed robe, painted bones, gold bangles and chain—every item he wore dripped blood. He approached the slaughter stone and showed the worshippers a feral grin, and his teeth glowed against the red blood.

Butterfly Wing stopped breathing.

The Jaguar raised a hand. He held no knife. His arm chopped down, and his flattened hand sliced into the chest of his victim, who thrashed briefly on the altar. The movement was effortless, the hand met no more resistance than if the priest dipped it in a vessel of water.

Butterfly Wing looked closely.

The priest's eyes turned green. The Jaguar's face changed, as if heat rising from a fire wavered the air around his head. His jaw opened to reveal long, cat-like fangs. He raised the hand. It held the victim's streaming heart. With a snarl, the priest bit into the blood muscle.

Butterfly Wing stepped away from the base of the temple, let the humans pass around him as though he waded backward through a river of flesh. He kept his eyes on the priest until he reached the edge of the crowd, and then he turned and walked away.

In that moment of the sacrifice's death he'd recognized the priest as Jaguar's Eye, a creature inhabited by the jaguar spirit, an entity as undying as Breath Of The Wind.

Butterfly Wing climbed the mountains out of the valley and headed out to the plains once more.


*400 AD – Cholula*

Something had happened.

Traveling by night, El Tigre had avoided capture since escaping Tenochtitlan. He had reached the foothills and was climbing slowly into the mountains surrounding the Valley of Mexico. He heard the small nocturnal creatures fleeing as he approached. He heard the call of an owl.

And suddenly he was blinking against the full blaze of day. He stood quietly and looked around. When the luchador realized what he was seeing, he took a seat on the ground and considered his situation.

A few steps ago, El Tigre had been climbing a rugged slope. Now he was on the other side of the mountain ridge, facing the plains outside the Valley of Mexico. And it was daytime. Was this more of Butterfly Wing's magic?

He shook his head. At least he'd been moved in the direction he wanted to go.

Wary, El Tigre descended the slope. He clung to tree boles where the incline was particularly steep.

He took three steps. The slope under his feet was gone. Instead, he stood among a stand of trees on a scrub-covered plain. The sun was midway between the eastern horizon—El Tigre guessed it was the east—and directly overhead. He took a breath, then he turned and surveyed the territory. He'd been flung somewhere else. Which direction? He didn't know. When in time was he? He didn't know that, either.

El Tigre walked forward five, six, seven steps. Slow, wary. An eighth step.

He was somewhere else again. The sun was far to the west—if the previous sun had indeed been in the east. And the terrain was rougher and more thickly timbered. El Tigre raised his eyes.

Towering before him was a cloud-haloed volcano.

Two volcanoes lay southeast of Mexico City: Popocatépetl and Iztaccíhuatl. The latter was dormant, but El Tigre didn't know if that had been true in whatever period he'd now been tossed. So he wasn't sure which one he now faced, and he hoped it wasn't due for an eruption.

Until he gained further information, San Lorenzo remained his destination. He set out fully expecting to be whisked off at any moment.

After an hour skirting the prominence with no interruptions, El Tigre was surprised when he took a sidestep to avoid a broken chunk of hardened lava and when his foot came down he found himself in a wide, paved plaza. A number of pyramidal structures studded the local landscape, each of a differing style and size from the others.

The luchador looked around. Behind him in the distance rose a smoking volcano—this one he felt sure to be Popocatépetl, which meant his current location was Cholula, home to a number of pyramids.

He still didn't know what time period currently held him. Nothing in his surroundings suggested he was any time close to home.

The people in the plaza who stared at this strange person who'd suddenly appeared were dressed like low-caste workers. Their responses varied: They dropped whatever they were carrying, or they pointed, goggle-eyed and gasping. Some shouted. Someone screamed.

*The past*, El Tigre thought, *is not welcoming.*

He didn't see an immediate threat, but he figured his best course would be to skedaddle out of town.

El Tigre was tired, but he waved his extended arms over his head and yelled in as fierce a voice he could manage. Hoping this display would discourage anyone from getting too close, he took off running for what looked like the closest edge of the community.

As he ran, something happened. Every few footfalls, the scenery changed, his shadow fell in a different direction, sometimes the daylight was gone entirely and he rushed through the night and hoped not to collide with something hidden in the dark. He ran just the same, and as he flickered helplessly from time to time and place to place, his bones jarred loose within his flesh, and his internal organs clashed and pulled in strange directions. His lungs heaved and he ran.

And then he stopped and fell to his knees and hands.

The sun blazed overhead and El Tigre was surrounded by yells and ululations and the crash of weapons. Two armies clashed around him. He was jostled and thrown to the ground. Light flashed from armor. He was among the Spanish conquistadores fighting the Aztecs!

The smell of blood and sweat filled the air. Men toppled over El Tigre. He pushed them aside and got to his feet. Consumed by their battle, to kill and to stay alive, no one seemed to notice him. He forced his way through the thrusting, swinging crowd as they jostled him and sprayed their blood on him. He could see no end to the soldiers and Aztec warriors.

A man swung a sword and its hilt dug into El Tigre's kidneys. Something else thumped the back of his head. He collapsed on the paving stones. The sounds pulsed and his sight swam in and out of focus.

El Tigre crawled. He struggled to his knees and inched forward. He didn't know if he was going deeper into the battle or heading toward its edges. He could concentrate only on one thing: *keep moving*. Exhausted and hardly thinking coherently by this point, he only had his gut feelings and whatever instinct for preservation remained. El Tigre felt that if he stopped moving, he would be trapped here.

He glanced up. Light flashing from armor dazzled his eyes. He blinked.

Everything went dark. And silent.

He still felt stone and grit under his bleeding palms and knees. After several moments, he realized he was wrong about the silence. He could hear low rhythms of insects and peeping tree frogs.

He sat and looked around. A moonless night was falling away and dawn's approaching light seeped into the sky. The stars faded as bird songs started and grew in number. He heard the bellow of a cow and the rattle of a goat's bell. Shapes began to grow more defined in the rising light.

The silhouettes of several hillocks surrounded El Tigre. Details emerged over the next several minutes. The hills were covered with trees and something else. When he could make out exactly what he was looking at, El Tigre knew where he was.

Each tree-bristled hillock was surmounted by a church or chapel. They had been built by the Spanish, centuries ago. And each hill was actually an earth-covered pyramid.

After flickering through multiple eras like a rock skipping across water, El Tigre recognized this place.

He was in Cholula once again. In his own time. *"Gracias a Dios."*


*1970 – Superstition Mountains, Arizona*

The silhouette of a man wearing a hat was suddenly framed in the cave opening, the day bright behind him.

"Hey," the figure said. "Hey, you're in here somewhere."

Silence.

"Hey," the figure said again, the voice a little raspy and carrying an unusual quality. "Hey, c'mon, I know you're here. You're not one of them." A pause. "You're one of us."

It took a moment, but Butterfly Wing stirred. He'd not done so for a long time.

The figure at the entrance didn't enter further to help. He waited until eventually Butterfly Wing shuffled to within a couple yards and leaned against the cave wall. Butterfly Wing worked up some spit and swallowed and managed to get his voice working. "I didn't hear you coming." He didn't speak English like the stranger. He used one of the old tongues from his days as a witch.

The man in the hat tilted his head. He answered in some language that wasn't English, but Breath Of The Wind understood it. "I can be quiet when I want to be."

Minutes passed between one man's utterance and that of the other, as if each weighed the other's words solemnly before responding. Butterfly Wing asked, "How did you know I was here?"

"I'm one of us, too." He held his face so the light revealed his profile, and his features looked like those of a dog. No, not a dog. A coyote.

He stepped outside fully into the sunlight and waved for Butterfly Wing to join him. His face was a man's face now, like that of the indigenous people who lived around here, and his hair was long and dark under the hat, which was a straw cowboy hat that had seen better days. He wore a long-sleeved shirt with the sleeves rolled above his elbows. It was a white shirt and it had mother-of-pearl buttons and a paisley yoke. He wore it with the tail out and hanging over faded blue jeans whose cuffs were frayed and bunched over a pair of scuffed brown work boots that hadn't been polished in a long time.

When Butterfly Wing passed from the line of the cave mouth's shadow into the sun, he trembled as he was struck by the light's brilliant hammers. The stranger reached but didn't touch, prepared to help if the cave dweller started to fall. Butterfly Wing moved his shoulders around and finally stood firm. He squinted in the direction of the sun and asked, "What's your name?"

"I have many names," came the answer, "depending on who is saying it and where that person may happen to be at the time. But you can call me Quixote. Odie for short." He gestured. "This way."

As Butterfly Wing began to follow along a game trail that led downward in a twisty manner along the flanks of the mountain and into erosion-chewed grooves cut into the soil, the last tattered rags of his clothing fell away. Without looking back, Odie called over his shoulder, "First off, we'll need to get you dressed. It's expected moreso these days."

The sun blew light at them from a different angle when they reached the base of the mountain. A dust-covered vehicle sat there, empty. Odie approached and leaned against its side and waited for Butterfly Wing to join him.

Breath Of The Wind studied the car through Butterfly Wing's eyes. It was blunt and streamlined in the ugly way humans made their objects. It was green. "What is this thing?"

Odie grinned and opened the trunk. "This is a gen-yoo-wine 1949 Hudson Commodore."

Butterfly Wind didn't understand this name, but he let the matter drop as he caught the items Odie tossed at him. He donned a shirt and jeans and was immediately irritated by the chafing they caused.

Odie grinned again as he shut the trunk lid with a satisfying *thunk* while his new companion growled at him. He waved away the threats and said, "Climb in."

Butterfly Wing sneered at the Hudson with suspicion, then approached one of the open windows and reached in. Odie grabbed a shoulder and pulled him back. "The passenger side. The other side. Like this." Butterfly Wing watched how Odie grasped the handle and opened the door. He went to the other side and repeated what he'd seen. The door opened. He sat on the cushioned seat and shut the door as Odie had done on his side. Butterfly Wing scowled. "It is hot."

"Just wait." Odie fiddled with the controls and gripped the circle the metal beast jutted toward him. The Hudson roared like a jungle monster and Butterfly Wing's hands latched on to whatever was closest. Odie laughed. "Sounds good, doesn't it? *Power.* C'mon, you'll cool off in a minute." The metal beast moved suddenly and the roar grew as the Hudson rolled along a barely-there two-wheel track through the dust and scrub. Wind flew in the window. After a mile or so, Breath Of The Wind relaxed his desperate grip and closed his eyes and opened his mouth for the rushing air to kiss him.

Odie looked at Butterfly Wing and laughed. He began to ask his passenger questions. Slowly at first, Butterfly Wing answered, then more boldly as he started to understand who his driver explained himself to be. He asked questions in response.

They reached a road covered with gravel that pinged and pecked against the Hudson's flanks. Eventually Odie drove on another road made with a single, long, black stone. Butterfly Wing watched through the windshield as it rushed toward them, then he turned and watched it run away behind them. "It's a paved road," Odie said. "Asphalt."

The sun was nearly gone when Odie stopped to feed the Hudson at a small building with a gas pump beside the paved road. Then they drove on until the sun had been replaced by darkness and the sky's million eyes. Odie drove several yards off and away from the edge of the pavement before stopping the car and killing the engine. "We'll rest here tonight." He reached in the back seat and brought forward two wool blankets. They smelled like sheep or goats. Butterfly Wing didn't want it, but he accepted it.

The two talked through the night while the sky performed its slow dance overhead. Their words continually shifted from English to old languages Breath Of The Wind had last heard when he had first joined the two-legged animals in the guise of Butterfly Wing and then on to a patois that was strange to Butterfly Wing but that he understood just the same. He told of his days before the humans and then of those periods when he lived among them and of the other times when he left them behind. He explained how he had tired of them and tried to escape their presence entirely by hiking to the north and finding the cave and remaining there.

Odie had nodded and asked further questions and commented occasionally. This was the pair's routine for the next two days—driving during the daylight, stopping at night, and conversing the entire time.

That third night, Odie said something that confused Butterfly Wind. "You've reached despair because you've been learning forward."

The two's conversation had been flowing among the various languages like water over and around stream stones, and Butterfly Wing thought he may have misunderstood. "I have been leaning forward?"

"No," Odie said and he uttered a short, barking laugh. "You've been *learning* forward. Moving only in one direction." He pointed to the stars. "We see their light. But it swam from their bodies generations ago. It's just now reached us. We perceive the light as if it is fresh and new, but it may be older than the moon."

"So?"

"You're living like the humans, in one direction only, at one moment at a time." Odie gestured vaguely. "Perhaps because you're inside that human." He dismissed the situation with a wave. "That is not for us. Time is everywhere, everywhen. All the time." He tapped a finger on Butterfly Wing's denim-covered knee. "That's how we work. That's how we play."

Fascinated, Breath Of The Wind finally recognized that elusive quality he'd first noticed in Odie's voice. It was the sound of someone who knew the person he was talking to didn't understand Odie was telling a joke. The tone never left Odie's voice.

For the first time since Breath Of The Wind usurped Butterfly Wing's life, he demonstrated humility. He said, "Teach me."

They set to it.

Attempting to experience time in more directions than just forward—that is, as he experienced it, in the way of the two-legged animals—was not so simple as Breath Of The Wind had imagined. Odie made suggestions, and then he sat and watched while Butterfly Wing closed one eye for several minutes, then closed the other eye for a similar length of time, and finally closed both eyes and concentrated on some event from his past. He strained against the invisible, intangible bonds he could barely comprehend. The resulting flatulence made his companion choke in the midst of his guffaws.

"C'mon, c'mon," Odie urged. "It's easy as falling off a bike."

Breath Of The Wind didn't understand Odie's meaning. Whatever he was supposed to be doing, easy didn't seem to be part of it.

Odie complained, "It's this meat suit you're wearing. It's holding you back."

Unaccustomed after years of solitude to hearing any words of criticism, Butterfly Wing replied in a stiff manner, "You wear the appearance of a human, too."

Odie shook his head and hissed. "People see what I want them to see. You rely on the human skin too much. You're too used to it."

Breath Of The Wind continued his silent striving. Despite the chill night air, sweat rolled from his skin.

After hours of this, he grew fatigued. He slowly relaxed, keeping in mind a particular event from his days in the Valley of Mexico. In one unexpected instant, he suddenly was falling forward. He extended his hands before him to keep from smashing his face on the ground, but with a start realized the ground wasn't there—he simply continued falling forward.

As he tumbled, the air was sucked from his ears. A sense of vertigo swallowed him. When his plunge stopped, he opened his eyes and the night's darkness was gone. He was again in Cholula and standing near its great stepped pyramid. The passersby paid him no mind as though the inexplicable appearance of strangers were a daily occurrence.

It had worked! His efforts to move back into the path of his time had succeeded.

He tried again. He closed his eyes and considered. Just as when he had started to flow from Odie's side, he had experienced a sense of sliding, as if he had slipped and lost his balance. Butterfly Wing silenced his mind and tried to bring back that off-balanced feeling.

There! A short inswept breath accompanied a moment of vertigo. He opened his eyes.

He stood among the trees beyond the plateau during the night in the days of the Red Palace. He listened to the owls and the whisper of leaves. He felt the humid breeze skim over his limbs. This was no dream. He was standing here just as he once had done—and now did so again.

Could he return to Odie's side? Or would this trick only allow him to travel backwards? Would he be trapped in the past?

He closed his eyes, thought about the unbalanced feeling of sliding—

—and found himself sitting on the ground under the sky beside Odie. His companion laughed and clapped his back. "Excellent! Hey, you did it, *niño!*" The next moment he pushed an open can of beer into Butterfly Wing's hand.

"Where did this come from?"

Odie opened another can with a church key that hung by a thong from a belt loop. "I made sure we had something to celebrate with." He turned up the can and drank a long moment from it. "Want to try again?"

Butterfly Wing nodded. He loosened his mind a bit, recaptured that sliding feeling, and leapt.

When he returned to Odie, no more than a second had passed since he had begun his journey. But while he was gone, he'd revisited many times and places. He delivered the bow and arrows he'd used to make Butterfly Wing a renowned hunter in the time of Dust In The Flower's Mouth and Flashing Rain In The Night—the mystery he'd faced when he'd first awakened and found the weapon by his sleeping mat, and his traditional darts missing, was now solved. He watched again as

Butterfly Wing trod homeward with the three birds he'd carried when Breath Of The Wind first invaded his body. He revisited Tenochtitlan and stayed long enough to whisper evil words about The Jaguar to envious and influential priests and to help them plot his capture. He skipped here and there through time and tasted again the worlds that had turned to dust as the humans experienced time. But Breath Of The Wind was no longer limited in this fashion.

He was free in a way he'd never imagined.


### *1974 – San Lorenzo, Mexico*

Three weeks after El Tigre Azul had met Jason Solomon Otterbridge and traveled to San Lorenzo, the luchador was heading there again. This time he was driving. In the passenger's seat was another luchador, Dr. Zaius. Although he also wore a mask, his wasn't the head-hugging sort that other luchadores wore. Dr. Zaius wore a gorilla mask.

After confirming he was back in his own time, El Tigre recuperated for a couple of days at a nearby farmhouse. He'd sent a message to Dr. Zaius, who'd arrived in the dented and crazy-quilt-painted Ford pickup El Tigre now drove.

"You know," Dr. Zaius said, "the ride is rougher over here than behind the wheel."

"You need new shocks."

"That's probably true." He gripped the front edge of the bench seat and the door handle. "What do you expect to find in San Lorenzo?"

The truck's bouncing made El Tigre's shrug impossible to detect. "If Butterfly Wing isn't still there, maybe a clue to where he's gone."

After eight hours of driving, El Tigre parked down the street from the warehouse where he'd met Butterfly Wing. It was after midnight. No radio or television noises floated along the street. No lights shone.

El Tigre and Dr. Zaius were alone with the sounds of insects and night birds and the ticking of the Ford's cooling engine.

Dr. Zaius rubbed his backside and stretched his back. "Gandhi's calluses!" he whispered. "I need a massage."

At the building's back corner, El Tigre told his friend, "Wait here. Ten minutes. If I'm not back out by then, peek in and check the situation."

"Then what?"

El Tigre paused, not sure how to answer. "Do what the situation calls for. But don't put yourself in danger."

At the door, El Tigre thought about everything he'd been through after he'd last entered this building. He took a deep breath and went in.

The place wasn't dark this time, but was filled with light. The bomb-making materials were gone. But a figure still sat in the far corner. Wary, El Tigre walked over to face the room's occupant. He asked, "Are you Butterfly Wing?"

"I am."

The man El Tigre last saw sitting in that chair had looked about forty years of age, healthy and fit. The man he now faced wore the same clothing, but appeared many decades older and seemed to be ailing.

"I sent the young ones away with their tools. Not at first," the old man said, "but when I was sure you would be returning."

El Tigre stood a few yards away from Butterfly Wing. He stayed balanced on the balls of his feet, ready for quick movement if the old man made a threatening move. "You didn't expect me to come back?"

"You were not supposed to," Butterfly Wing admitted. "You are resilient. Like all the two-legged animals. Resilient." The old man waved a hand in a feeble gesture, and El Tigre nearly leaped on him, but he held his place when Butterfly Wing continued talking. "The young people told me about you. They said you have a history of strange encounters. What they told me," he shook his head, "I think explains why you came back."

El Tigre waited for the old man to continue. Finally he asked, "Well?"

Butterfly Wing took a few breaths. "What I did to you should have killed you. No man is prepared for what happened to you. But you are here."

"Here I am."

Butterfly Wing nodded. "Your strange encounters have made you resilient in a way I have not seen before. I can fly through the past with no effort. Putting you there—no effort." His shoulders slumped. "Keeping you there," he said. He repeated, "Keeping you there," and his expression turned fierce and he glared at the luchador, "was a battle."

The energy the old man had put into his scowl seemed to have exhausted him. He panted.

"I am not so strong for this type of thing," he said after catching his breath.

The light flickered and went out.

El Tigre lunged to the side. He hit the floor and rolled and then landed on his feet. He listened for a telltale sound from Butterfly Wing.

The door behind El Tigre swung open and a flashlight beam broke through the darkness. Dr. Zaius called, "Blue Tiger?"

The beam landed on Butterfly Wing's chair. It held only a puddle of clothing. A curl of dust rose from the seat and turned in the air disturbed by the opened door.

El Tigre said, "I'm here." He'd paused before answering. He thought he'd heard something right after Dr. Zaius' call. A sigh of the wind. Almost like a voice. A whisper: *"Liberadooooooo."*

*Coda: 1974 – Durango, Mexico*

El Tigre Azul had retreated to the highlands in Durango for much-needed rest. He packed his necessities into the rugged mountains on foot. He fished, he watched the birds, he gazed at the stars while they turned slowly through the sky from horizon to horizon during the night. In the afternoons, he read a paperback copy of *En los bajos del Majestic*, by Georges Simenon, in the shade of a pine tree.

He liked how Inspector Maigret brought order to a disrupted world. No theatrics, no dramatic showdowns. Just a pipe, a beer, and the patience to let people reveal themselves. El Tigre found it calming and reassuring.

The third day after making his camp, El Tigre sat up from reading his book and listened. The birds had gone silent. So had the insects' snicketing and burring. In the sudden quiet, El Tigre heard a vigorous rush of wind. The luchador looked around. Despite the sound, the grass didn't bend and the tree limbs didn't sway. He turned his head this way and that. What was going on?

The blowing sound got louder. Closer.

With a rush, the book was snatched from his hand. He watched as it tumbled through the air, flying away, the pages rattling and flapping. El Tigre stood. The book disappeared around the shoulder of the hill.

The rushing sound diminished and died.

# { 4 }

# The Expanded Edition

I first published the first story in this collection, "Three Witches (*Tres Brujas*)," as an ebook in 2012. At the time, it was the longest piece of fiction I'd written.

During the following years, as I wrote and published other stories, a number of people mentioned how they'd enjoyed the story and the character of El Tigre Azul. They also mentioned they'd like to read more about him. Other folks said they'd like to read about him, but they preferred to read physical books instead of electronic books.

I eventually decided I wanted to write more of El Tigre's adventures and to give readers an opportunity to read them in whichever format they preferred. The result is this book. It's called an "expanded edition" because if features a slightly revised version of the original story plus two new tales. Each story features one or another type of witch, so the ebook's original title still rings true: three adventures with at least one witch in each.

More El Tigre tales remain to be told. One story featuring a character who appears in this book, El Puño de Bronce, already exists in *Restless:*

*An Anthology of Mummy Horror*, a collection published by Flinch Books. That story, "Whispers from the Dread World," has a connection to one of the new stories included in the volume you're now reading.

I like El Tigre. I look forward to sharing more stories about him. If you've enjoyed this expanded edition, please let me know through the links listed below. I look forward to hearing your responses.

# ABOUT THE AUTHOR

Coming from a long line of long-winded tall tale tellers, Duane Spurlock loves good storytelling. A professional writer since the last century, Duane writes adventure tales informed by a lifetime of omnivorous reading and studying great storytellers.

Duane has contributed to various fiction and nonfiction anthologies. In addition to his own titles, he is the co-author, with Jim Beard, of *Airship Hunters*, an 1897 action-mystery based on actual newspaper reports about strange objects flying in the skies of western North America. You can learn more about Duane and his books and sign up for updates at www.duanespurlock.com.

# ABOUT THE COVER ARTIST

Jeffrey Ray Hayes is a freelance illustrator and graphic designer living in the Austin metro area of Central Texas. Jeff has worked in the art department on several indie television / web-based productions and indie films in the United States and United Kingdom, creating promotional materials and key art for entertainment industry marketing. His primary focus is book cover illustration and visual marketing for authors, and has completed over 250 pieces that have graced the covers of various books and magazines. Learn more about Jeff and his work at www.plasmafiregraphics.com.

Made in the USA
Middletown, DE
26 May 2023

31550503R00130